# THE ADVENTURES OF THE GRAND VIZIER IZNOGOUD
## BY GOSCINNY & TABARY

# IZNOGOUD
## ROCKETS TO STARDOM

**SCRIPT: GOSCINNY**          **DRAWING: TABARY**

9th CINEBOOK
The 9th Art Publisher

Original title: Des astres pour Iznogoud

Original edition: © Dargaud Editeur Paris, 1969, by Goscinny & Tabary
www.dargaud.com

Lettering and text layout: Imadjinn sarl
Printed in Spain by Just Colour Graphic

This edition published in Great Britain in 2011 by
Cinebook Ltd
56 Beech Avenue,
Canterbury, Kent
CT4 7TA
www.cinebook.com

A CIP catalogue record for this book
is available from the British Library

978-1-84918-092-4

THERE WAS IN BAGHDAD THE MAGNIFICENT A GRAND VIZIER (5 FEET TALL IN HIS POINTY SLIPPERS) NAMED IZNOGOUD. HE WAS TRULY NASTY AND HAD ONLY ONE GOAL...

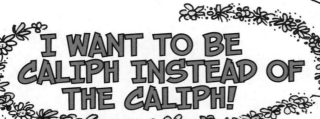

I WANT TO BE CALIPH INSTEAD OF THE CALIPH!

I WANT TO BE CALIPH INSTEAD OF THE CALIPH!

I WANT TO BE CALIPH INSTEAD OF THE CALIPH!

THIS VILE, NARROW-MINDED GRAND VIZIER HAD A FAITHFUL STRONG-ARM MAN NAMED WA'AT ALAHF. THIS FELLOW, DESPITE HIS NAME, DIDN'T LAUGH VERY OFTEN.

ALWAYS FOR PHOTOS.

WHILE THE CALIPH OF BAGHDAD, THE GOOD HAROUN AL PLASSID, WHO HAD ABSOLUTE CONFIDENCE IN HIS GRAND VIZIER, PASSED HIS HAPPY, SLEEPY DAYS IN THE SWEET SERENITY OF HIS SOVEREIGNTY.

I AM AT PEACE.

TABARY

NOW THEN, TO BAGHDAD THE MAGNIFICENT...

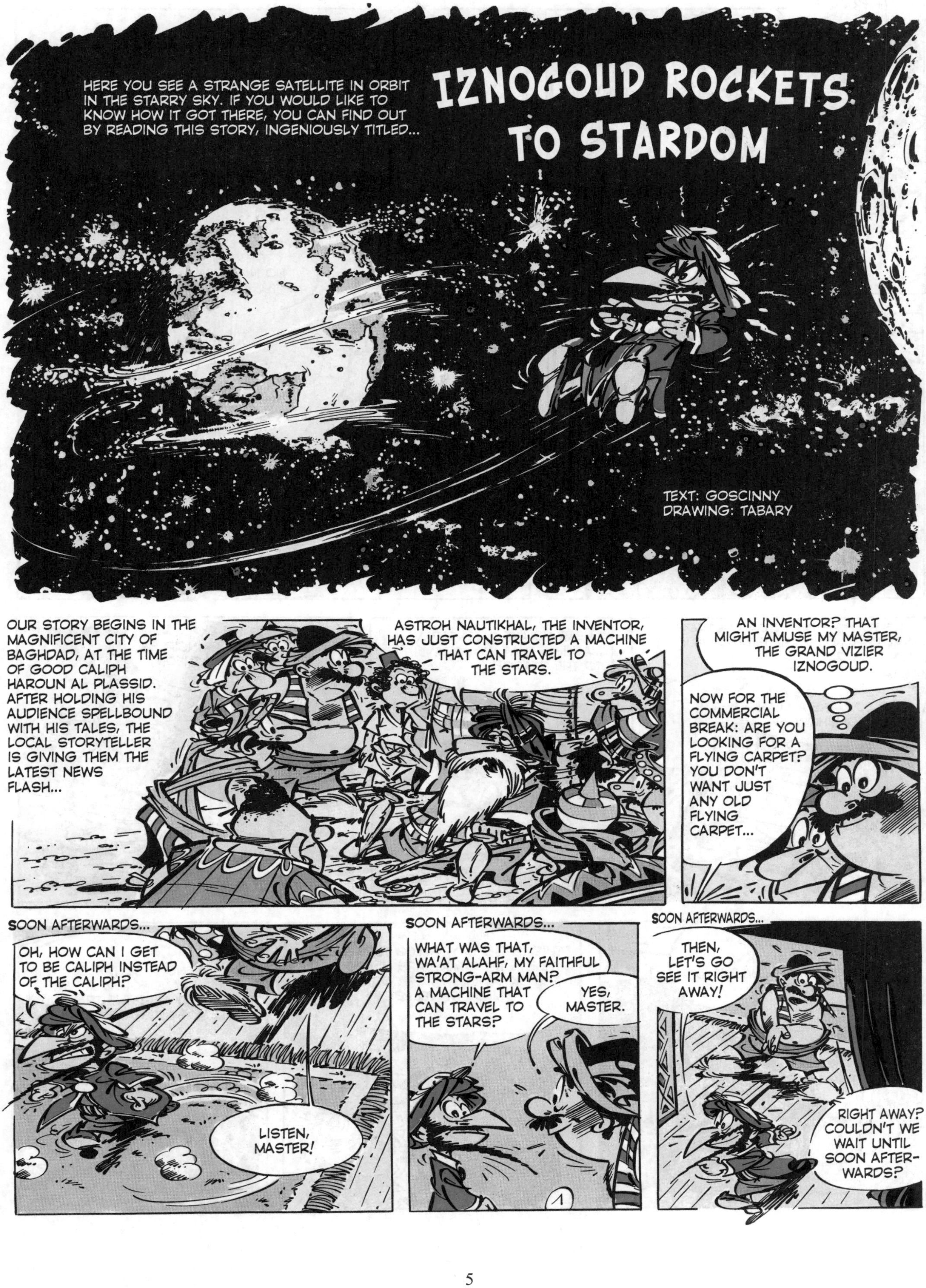
HERE YOU SEE A STRANGE SATELLITE IN ORBIT IN THE STARRY SKY. IF YOU WOULD LIKE TO KNOW HOW IT GOT THERE, YOU CAN FIND OUT BY READING THIS STORY, INGENIOUSLY TITLED...
IZNOGOUD ROCKETS TO STARDOM
TEXT: GOSCINNY
DRAWING: TABARY
OUR STORY BEGINS IN THE MAGNIFICENT CITY OF BAGHDAD, AT THE TIME OF GOOD CALIPH HAROUN AL PLASSID. AFTER HOLDING HIS AUDIENCE SPELLBOUND WITH HIS TALES, THE LOCAL STORYTELLER IS GIVING THEM THE LATEST NEWS FLASH...
ASTROH NAUTIKHAL, THE INVENTOR, HAS JUST CONSTRUCTED A MACHINE THAT CAN TRAVEL TO THE STARS.
NOW FOR THE COMMERCIAL BREAK: ARE YOU LOOKING FOR A FLYING CARPET? YOU DON'T WANT JUST ANY OLD FLYING CARPET...
AN INVENTOR? THAT MIGHT AMUSE MY MASTER, THE GRAND VIZIER IZNOGOUD.
SOON AFTERWARDS...
OH, HOW CAN I GET TO BE CALIPH INSTEAD OF THE CALIPH?
LISTEN, MASTER!
SOON AFTERWARDS...
WHAT WAS THAT, WA'AT ALAHF, MY FAITHFUL STRONG-ARM MAN? A MACHINE THAT CAN TRAVEL TO THE STARS?
YES, MASTER.
SOON AFTERWARDS...
THEN, LET'S GO SEE IT RIGHT AWAY!
RIGHT AWAY? COULDN'T WE WAIT UNTIL SOON AFTER-WARDS?

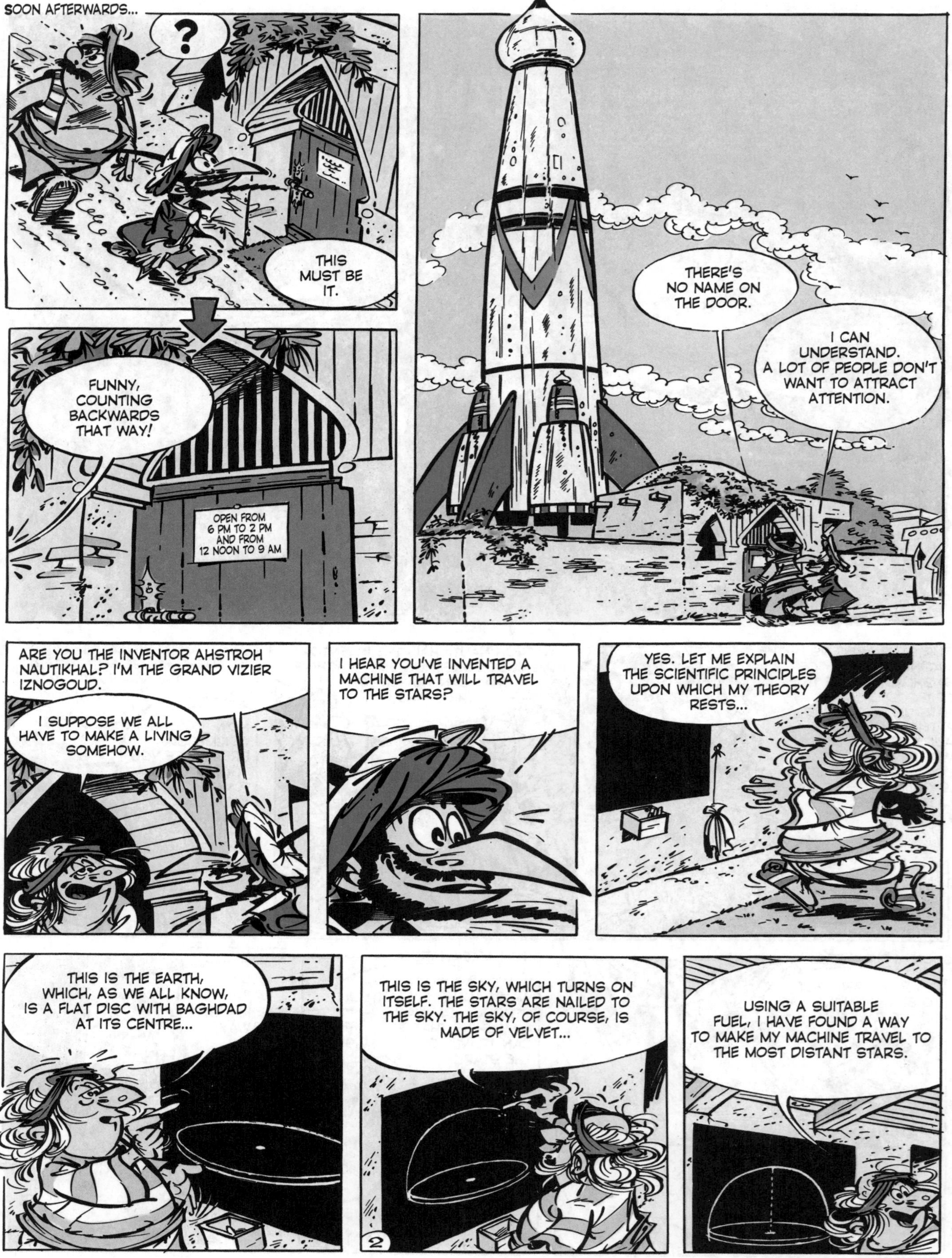
SOON AFTERWARDS...
?
THIS MUST BE IT.
FUNNY, COUNTING BACKWARDS THAT WAY!
OPEN FROM 6 PM TO 2 PM AND FROM 12 NOON TO 9 AM
THERE'S NO NAME ON THE DOOR.
I CAN UNDERSTAND. A LOT OF PEOPLE DON'T WANT TO ATTRACT ATTENTION.
ARE YOU THE INVENTOR AHSTROH NAUTIKHAL? I'M THE GRAND VIZIER IZNOGOUD.
I SUPPOSE WE ALL HAVE TO MAKE A LIVING SOMEHOW.
I HEAR YOU'VE INVENTED A MACHINE THAT WILL TRAVEL TO THE STARS?
YES. LET ME EXPLAIN THE SCIENTIFIC PRINCIPLES UPON WHICH MY THEORY RESTS...
THIS IS THE EARTH, WHICH, AS WE ALL KNOW, IS A FLAT DISC WITH BAGHDAD AT ITS CENTRE...
THIS IS THE SKY, WHICH TURNS ON ITSELF. THE STARS ARE NAILED TO THE SKY. THE SKY, OF COURSE, IS MADE OF VELVET...
USING A SUITABLE FUEL, I HAVE FOUND A WAY TO MAKE MY MACHINE TRAVEL TO THE MOST DISTANT STARS.

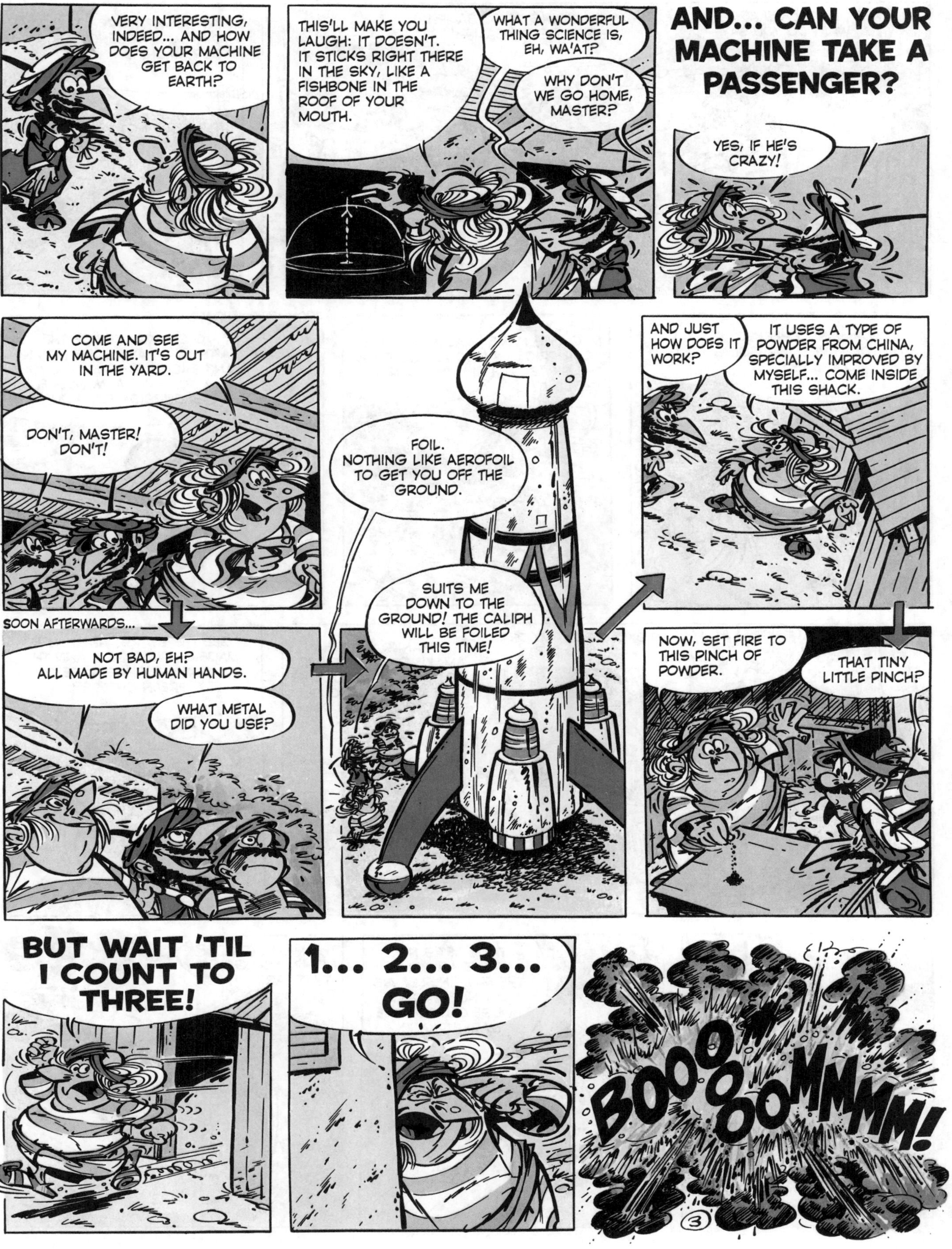

VERY INTERESTING, INDEED... AND HOW DOES YOUR MACHINE GET BACK TO EARTH?
THIS'LL MAKE YOU LAUGH: IT DOESN'T. IT STICKS RIGHT THERE IN THE SKY, LIKE A FISHBONE IN THE ROOF OF YOUR MOUTH.
WHAT A WONDERFUL THING SCIENCE IS, EH, WA'AT?
WHY DON'T WE GO HOME, MASTER?
AND... CAN YOUR MACHINE TAKE A PASSENGER?
YES, IF HE'S CRAZY!
COME AND SEE MY MACHINE. IT'S OUT IN THE YARD.
DON'T, MASTER! DON'T!
SOON AFTERWARDS...
NOT BAD, EH? ALL MADE BY HUMAN HANDS.
WHAT METAL DID YOU USE?
FOIL. NOTHING LIKE AEROFOIL TO GET YOU OFF THE GROUND.
SUITS ME DOWN TO THE GROUND! THE CALIPH WILL BE FOILED THIS TIME!
AND JUST HOW DOES IT WORK?
IT USES A TYPE OF POWDER FROM CHINA, SPECIALLY IMPROVED BY MYSELF... COME INSIDE THIS SHACK.
NOW, SET FIRE TO THIS PINCH OF POWDER.
THAT TINY LITTLE PINCH?
BUT WAIT 'TIL I COUNT TO THREE!
1... 2... 3... GO!
BOOOOOOOMMMMMM!

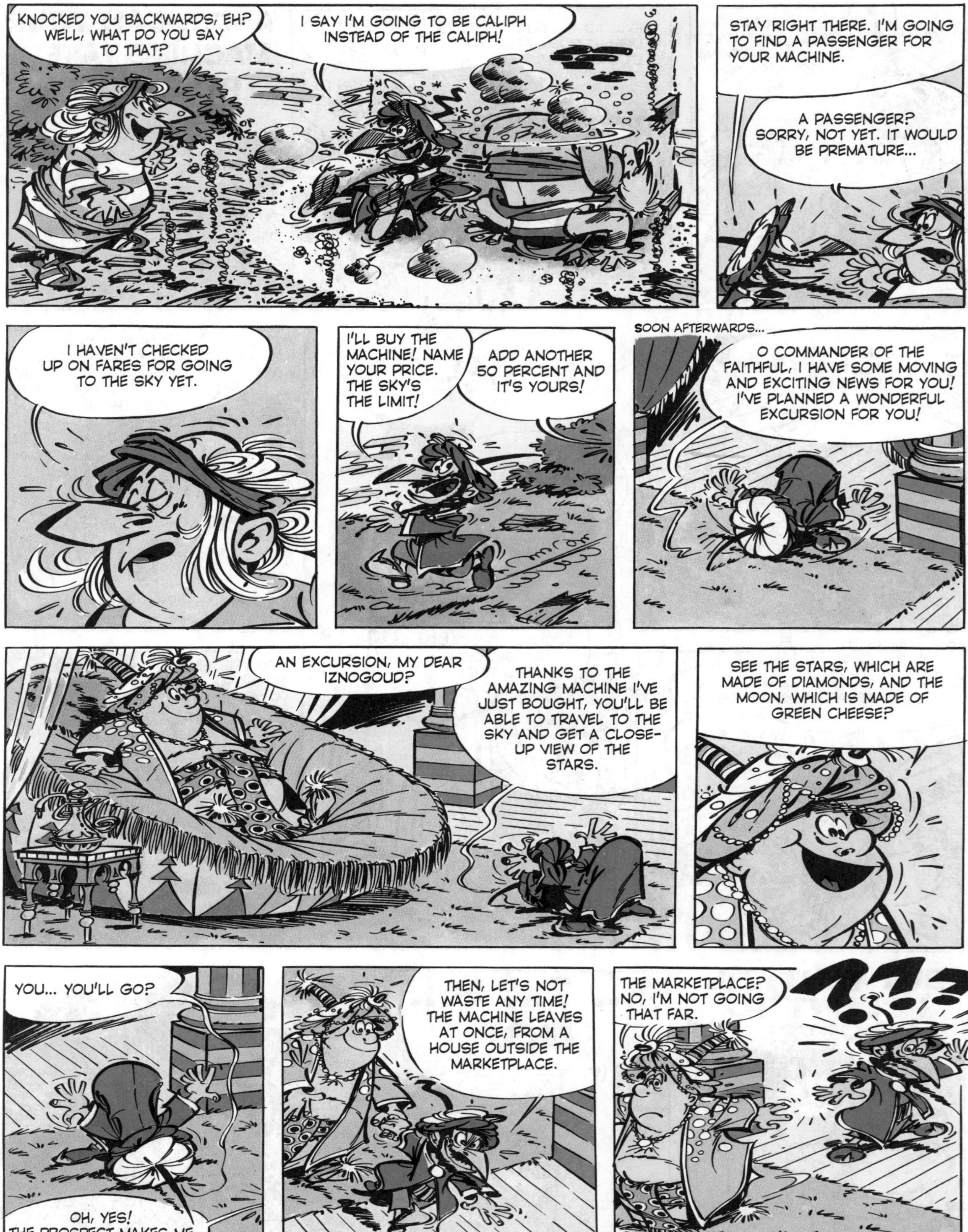
KNOCKED YOU BACKWARDS, EH? WELL, WHAT DO YOU SAY TO THAT?
I SAY I'M GOING TO BE CALIPH INSTEAD OF THE CALIPH!
STAY RIGHT THERE. I'M GOING TO FIND A PASSENGER FOR YOUR MACHINE.
A PASSENGER? SORRY, NOT YET. IT WOULD BE PREMATURE...
I HAVEN'T CHECKED UP ON FARES FOR GOING TO THE SKY YET.
I'LL BUY THE MACHINE! NAME YOUR PRICE. THE SKY'S THE LIMIT!
ADD ANOTHER 50 PERCENT AND IT'S YOURS!
SOON AFTERWARDS...
O COMMANDER OF THE FAITHFUL, I HAVE SOME MOVING AND EXCITING NEWS FOR YOU! I'VE PLANNED A WONDERFUL EXCURSION FOR YOU!
AN EXCURSION, MY DEAR IZNOGOUD?
THANKS TO THE AMAZING MACHINE I'VE JUST BOUGHT, YOU'LL BE ABLE TO TRAVEL TO THE SKY AND GET A CLOSE-UP VIEW OF THE STARS.
SEE THE STARS, WHICH ARE MADE OF DIAMONDS, AND THE MOON, WHICH IS MADE OF GREEN CHEESE?
YOU... YOU'LL GO?
OH, YES! THE PROSPECT MAKES ME QUITE STARRY-EYED!
THEN, LET'S NOT WASTE ANY TIME! THE MACHINE LEAVES AT ONCE, FROM A HOUSE OUTSIDE THE MARKETPLACE.
THE MARKETPLACE? NO, I'M NOT GOING THAT FAR.
???
4

**YOU DON'T MIND GOING TO THE MOON, BUT YOU WON'T WALK AS FAR AS BAGHDAD MARKETPLACE??**

THAT'S RIGHT. I WOULDN'T BE WALKING TO THE MOON.

OKAY. OKAY. I'LL HAVE THE MACHINE BROUGHT TO THE PALACE.

SOON AFTERWARDS...

GOING TO THE MOON IS ONE THING; GOING TO THE PALACE IS ANOTHER... THAT MACHINE OF YOURS IS HEAVY.

I'VE BROUGHT A FLEET OF SHIPS OF THE DESERT TO PULL IT ALONG.

SOON AFTERWARDS...

I'M A BIT WORRIED... THE SUN'S BEATING DOWN ON THAT MACHINE.

SO WHAT?

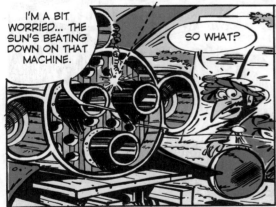

WELL, I'M NOT QUITE SURE HOW MY SPECIALLY IMPROVED POWDER WILL REACT TO THE HEAT...

BRRRRROO... OOOMM

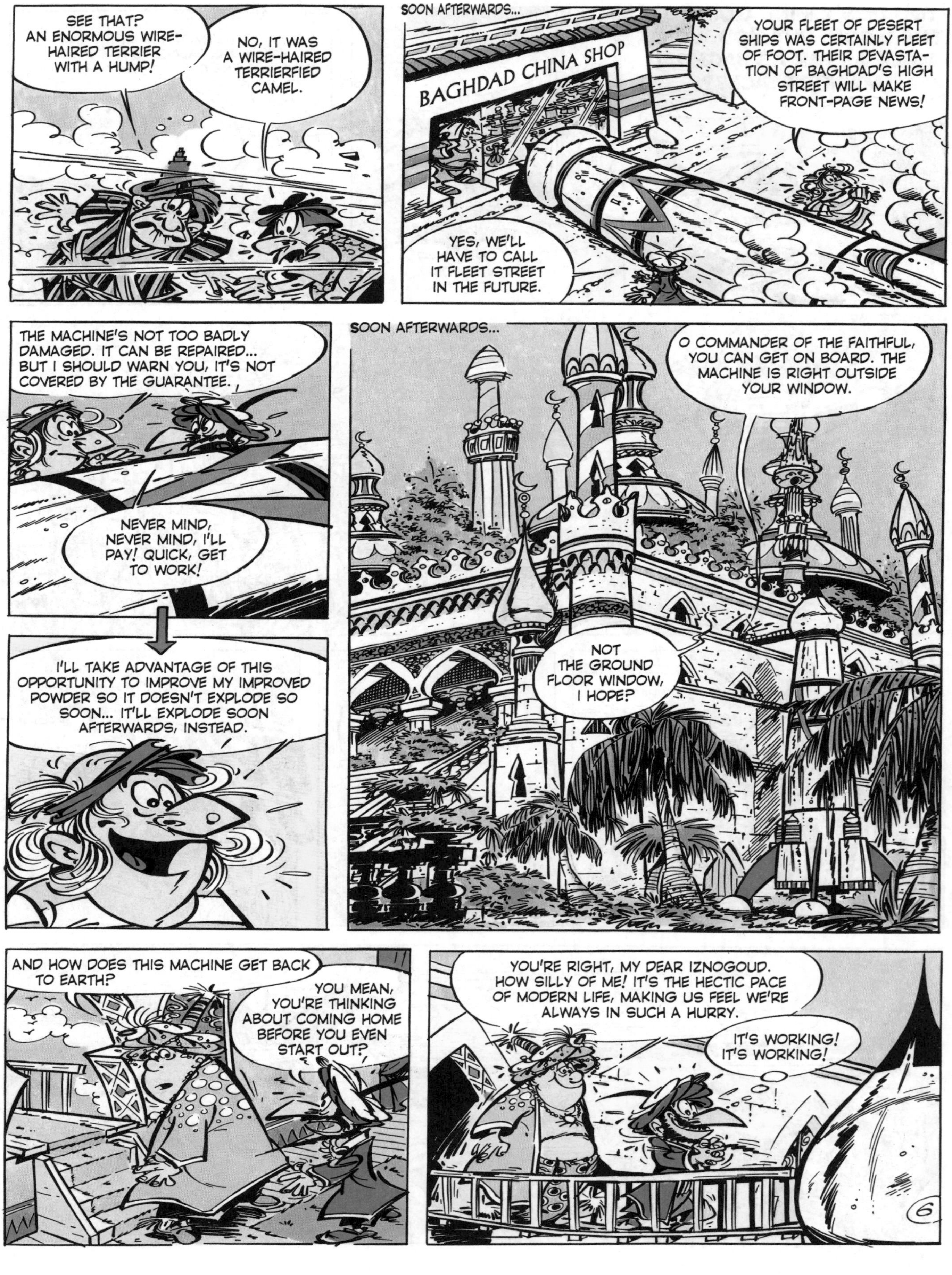
SEE THAT? AN ENORMOUS WIRE-HAIRED TERRIER WITH A HUMP!
NO, IT WAS A WIRE-HAIRED TERRIERFIED CAMEL.
SOON AFTERWARDS...
BAGHDAD CHINA SHOP
YOUR FLEET OF DESERT SHIPS WAS CERTAINLY FLEET OF FOOT. THEIR DEVASTATION OF BAGHDAD'S HIGH STREET WILL MAKE FRONT-PAGE NEWS!
YES, WE'LL HAVE TO CALL IT FLEET STREET IN THE FUTURE.
THE MACHINE'S NOT TOO BADLY DAMAGED. IT CAN BE REPAIRED... BUT I SHOULD WARN YOU, IT'S NOT COVERED BY THE GUARANTEE.
NEVER MIND, NEVER MIND, I'LL PAY! QUICK, GET TO WORK!
I'LL TAKE ADVANTAGE OF THIS OPPORTUNITY TO IMPROVE MY IMPROVED POWDER SO IT DOESN'T EXPLODE SO SOON... IT'LL EXPLODE SOON AFTERWARDS, INSTEAD.
SOON AFTERWARDS...
O COMMANDER OF THE FAITHFUL, YOU CAN GET ON BOARD. THE MACHINE IS RIGHT OUTSIDE YOUR WINDOW.
NOT THE GROUND FLOOR WINDOW, I HOPE?
AND HOW DOES THIS MACHINE GET BACK TO EARTH?
YOU MEAN, YOU'RE THINKING ABOUT COMING HOME BEFORE YOU EVEN START OUT?
YOU'RE RIGHT, MY DEAR IZNOGOUD. HOW SILLY OF ME! IT'S THE HECTIC PACE OF MODERN LIFE, MAKING US FEEL WE'RE ALWAYS IN SUCH A HURRY.
IT'S WORKING! IT'S WORKING!
6

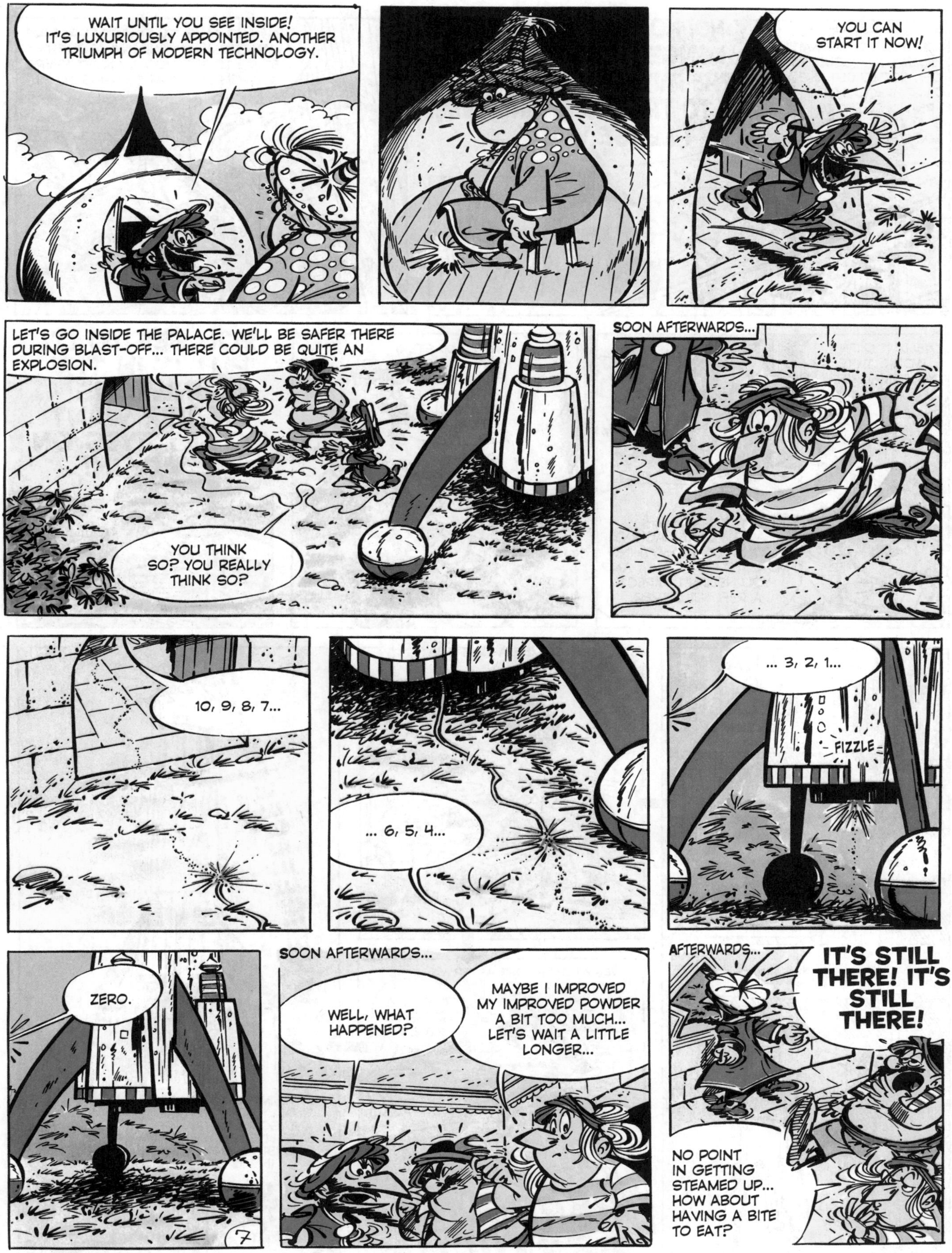
WAIT UNTIL YOU SEE INSIDE! IT'S LUXURIOUSLY APPOINTED. ANOTHER TRIUMPH OF MODERN TECHNOLOGY.
YOU CAN START IT NOW!
LET'S GO INSIDE THE PALACE. WE'LL BE SAFER THERE DURING BLAST-OFF... THERE COULD BE QUITE AN EXPLOSION.
YOU THINK SO? YOU REALLY THINK SO?
SOON AFTERWARDS...
10, 9, 8, 7...
... 6, 5, 4...
... 3, 2, 1...
FIZZLE
ZERO.
7
SOON AFTERWARDS...
WELL, WHAT HAPPENED?
MAYBE I IMPROVED MY IMPROVED POWDER A BIT TOO MUCH... LET'S WAIT A LITTLE LONGER...
AFTERWARDS...
IT'S STILL THERE! IT'S STILL THERE!
NO POINT IN GETTING STEAMED UP... HOW ABOUT HAVING A BITE TO EAT?

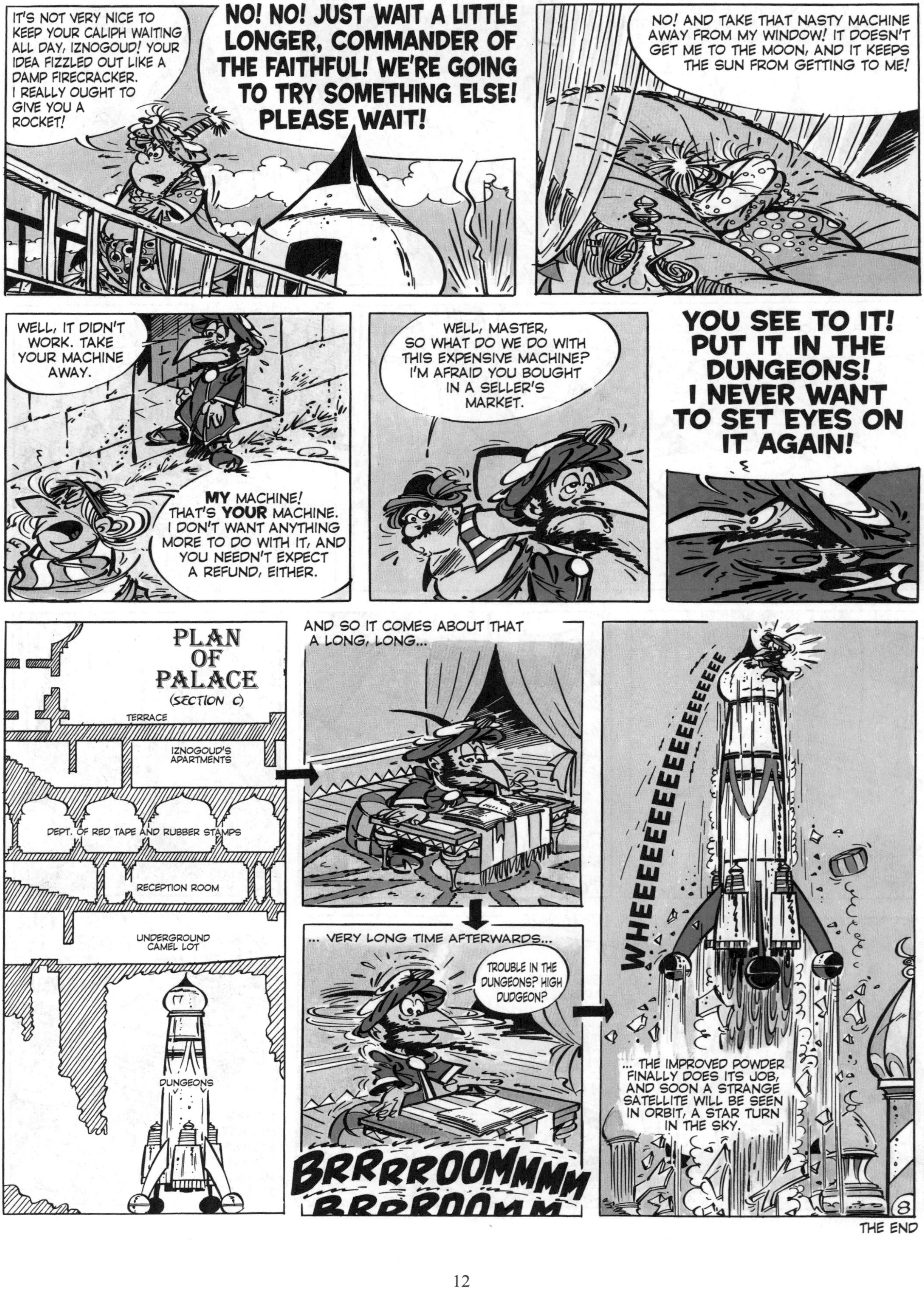
IT'S NOT VERY NICE TO KEEP YOUR CALIPH WAITING ALL DAY, IZNOGOUD! YOUR IDEA FIZZLED OUT LIKE A DAMP FIRECRACKER. I REALLY OUGHT TO GIVE YOU A ROCKET!
NO! NO! JUST WAIT A LITTLE LONGER, COMMANDER OF THE FAITHFUL! WE'RE GOING TO TRY SOMETHING ELSE! PLEASE WAIT!
NO! AND TAKE THAT NASTY MACHINE AWAY FROM MY WINDOW! IT DOESN'T GET ME TO THE MOON, AND IT KEEPS THE SUN FROM GETTING TO ME!
WELL, IT DIDN'T WORK. TAKE YOUR MACHINE AWAY.
MY MACHINE! THAT'S YOUR MACHINE. I DON'T WANT ANYTHING MORE TO DO WITH IT, AND YOU NEEDN'T EXPECT A REFUND, EITHER.
WELL, MASTER, SO WHAT DO WE DO WITH THIS EXPENSIVE MACHINE? I'M AFRAID YOU BOUGHT IN A SELLER'S MARKET.
YOU SEE TO IT! PUT IT IN THE DUNGEONS! I NEVER WANT TO SET EYES ON IT AGAIN!
PLAN OF PALACE
(SECTION C)
TERRACE
IZNOGOUD'S APARTMENTS
DEPT. OF RED TAPE AND RUBBER STAMPS
RECEPTION ROOM
UNDERGROUND CAMEL LOT
DUNGEONS
AND SO IT COMES ABOUT THAT A LONG, LONG...
... VERY LONG TIME AFTERWARDS...
TROUBLE IN THE DUNGEONS? HIGH DUDGEON?
BRRRROOMMMM
BRRROOMM
WHEEEEEEEEEEEEEE
... THE IMPROVED POWDER FINALLY DOES ITS JOB, AND SOON A STRANGE SATELLITE WILL BE SEEN IN ORBIT, A STAR TURN IN THE SKY.
8

THE END

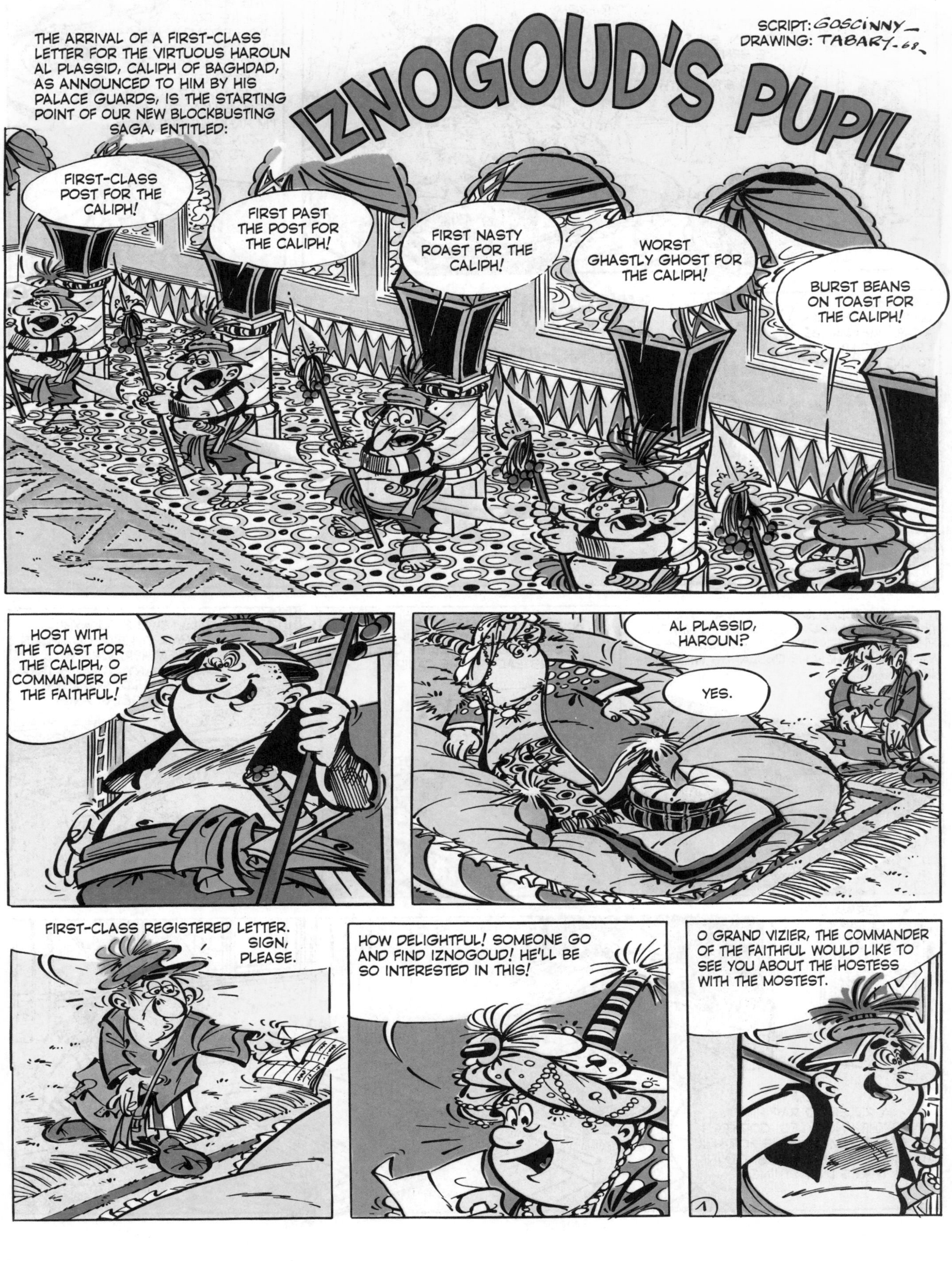
SCRIPT: GOSCINNY
DRAWING: TABARY 68
THE ARRIVAL OF A FIRST-CLASS LETTER FOR THE VIRTUOUS HAROUN AL PLASSID, CALIPH OF BAGHDAD, AS ANNOUNCED TO HIM BY HIS PALACE GUARDS, IS THE STARTING POINT OF OUR NEW BLOCKBUSTING SAGA, ENTITLED:
IZNOGOUD'S PUPIL
FIRST-CLASS POST FOR THE CALIPH!
FIRST PAST THE POST FOR THE CALIPH!
FIRST NASTY ROAST FOR THE CALIPH!
WORST GHASTLY GHOST FOR THE CALIPH!
BURST BEANS ON TOAST FOR THE CALIPH!
HOST WITH THE TOAST FOR THE CALIPH, O COMMANDER OF THE FAITHFUL!
AL PLASSID, HAROUN?
YES.
FIRST-CLASS REGISTERED LETTER. SIGN, PLEASE.
HOW DELIGHTFUL! SOMEONE GO AND FIND IZNOGOUD! HE'LL BE SO INTERESTED IN THIS!
O GRAND VIZIER, THE COMMANDER OF THE FAITHFUL WOULD LIKE TO SEE YOU ABOUT THE HOSTESS WITH THE MOSTEST.

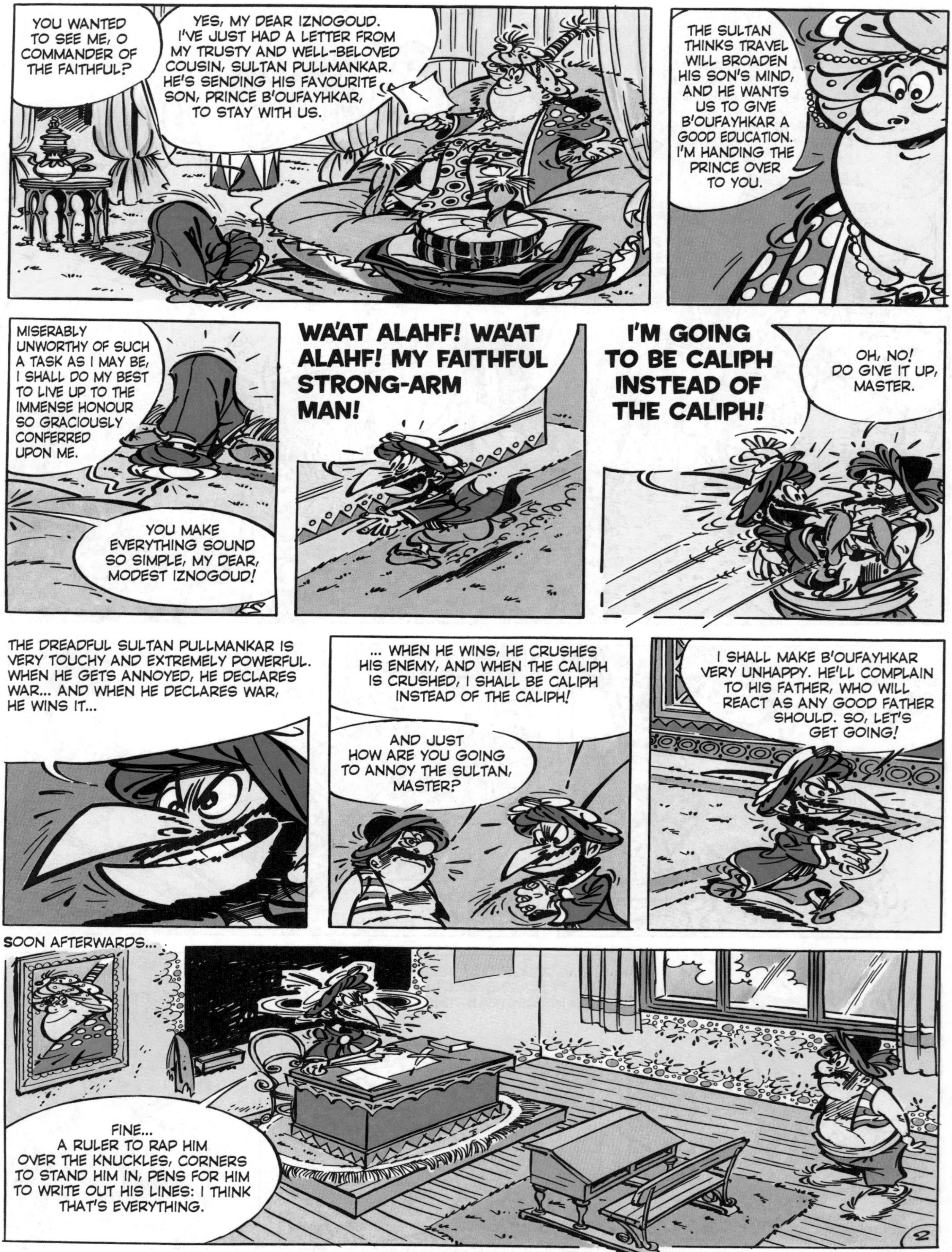

YOU WANTED TO SEE ME, O COMMANDER OF THE FAITHFUL?
YES, MY DEAR IZNOGOUD. I'VE JUST HAD A LETTER FROM MY TRUSTY AND WELL-BELOVED COUSIN, SULTAN PULLMANKAR. HE'S SENDING HIS FAVOURITE SON, PRINCE B'OUFAYHKAR, TO STAY WITH US.
THE SULTAN THINKS TRAVEL WILL BROADEN HIS SON'S MIND, AND HE WANTS US TO GIVE B'OUFAYHKAR A GOOD EDUCATION. I'M HANDING THE PRINCE OVER TO YOU.
MISERABLY UNWORTHY OF SUCH A TASK AS I MAY BE, I SHALL DO MY BEST TO LIVE UP TO THE IMMENSE HONOUR SO GRACIOUSLY CONFERRED UPON ME.
YOU MAKE EVERYTHING SOUND SO SIMPLE, MY DEAR, MODEST IZNOGOUD!
WA'AT ALAHF! WA'AT ALAHF! MY FAITHFUL STRONG-ARM MAN!
I'M GOING TO BE CALIPH INSTEAD OF THE CALIPH!
OH, NO! DO GIVE IT UP, MASTER.
THE DREADFUL SULTAN PULLMANKAR IS VERY TOUCHY AND EXTREMELY POWERFUL. WHEN HE GETS ANNOYED, HE DECLARES WAR... AND WHEN HE DECLARES WAR, HE WINS IT...
... WHEN HE WINS, HE CRUSHES HIS ENEMY, AND WHEN THE CALIPH IS CRUSHED, I SHALL BE CALIPH INSTEAD OF THE CALIPH!
AND JUST HOW ARE YOU GOING TO ANNOY THE SULTAN, MASTER?
I SHALL MAKE B'OUFAYHKAR VERY UNHAPPY. HE'LL COMPLAIN TO HIS FATHER, WHO WILL REACT AS ANY GOOD FATHER SHOULD. SO, LET'S GET GOING!
SOON AFTERWARDS...
FINE... A RULER TO RAP HIM OVER THE KNUCKLES, CORNERS TO STAND HIM IN, PENS FOR HIM TO WRITE OUT HIS LINES: I THINK THAT'S EVERYTHING.

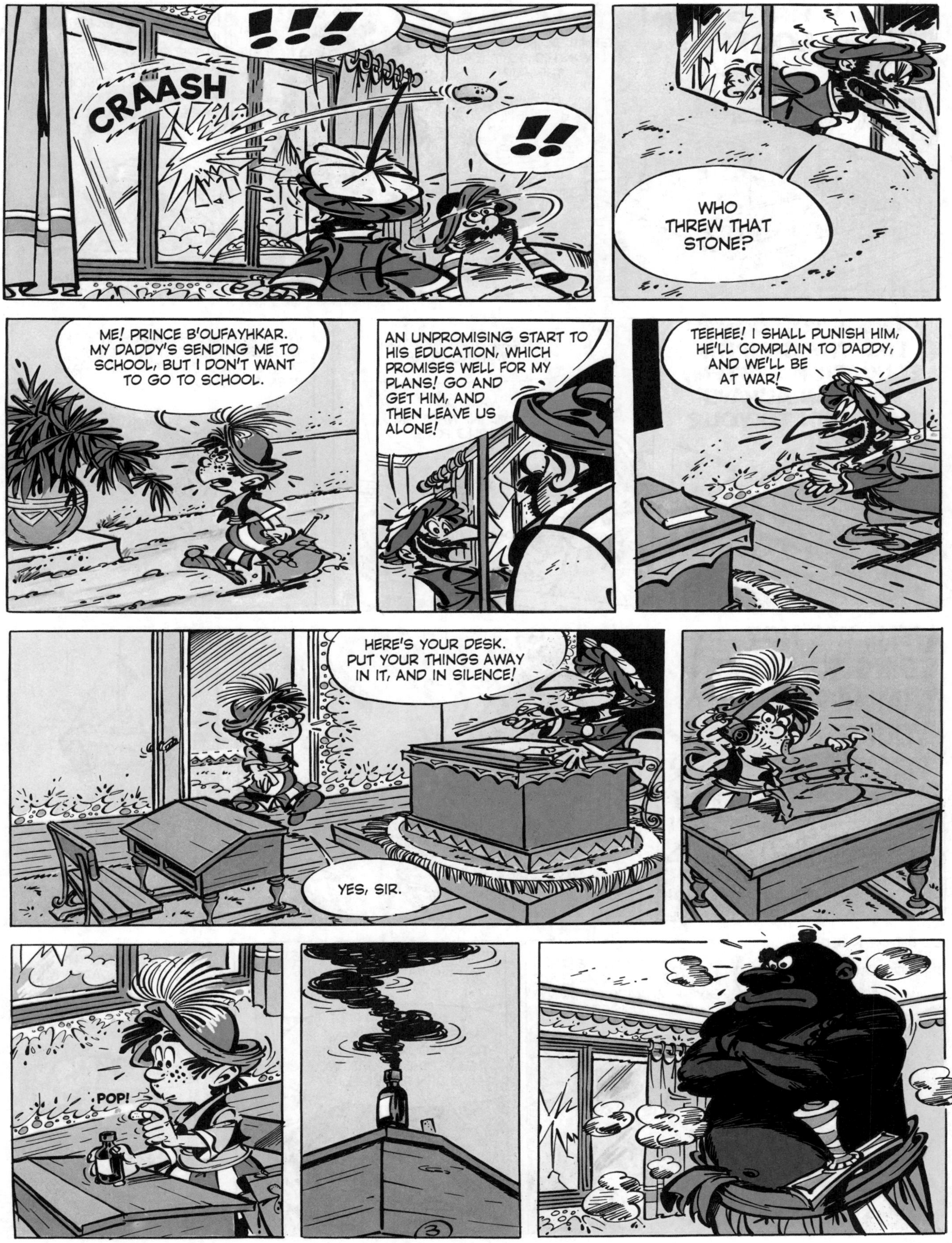
!!!
CRAASH
!!
WHO THREW THAT STONE?
ME! PRINCE B'OUFAYHKAR. MY DADDY'S SENDING ME TO SCHOOL, BUT I DON'T WANT TO GO TO SCHOOL.
AN UNPROMISING START TO HIS EDUCATION, WHICH PROMISES WELL FOR MY PLANS! GO AND GET HIM, AND THEN LEAVE US ALONE!
TEEHEE! I SHALL PUNISH HIM, HE'LL COMPLAIN TO DADDY, AND WE'LL BE AT WAR!
HERE'S YOUR DESK. PUT YOUR THINGS AWAY IN IT, AND IN SILENCE!
YES, SIR.
POP!

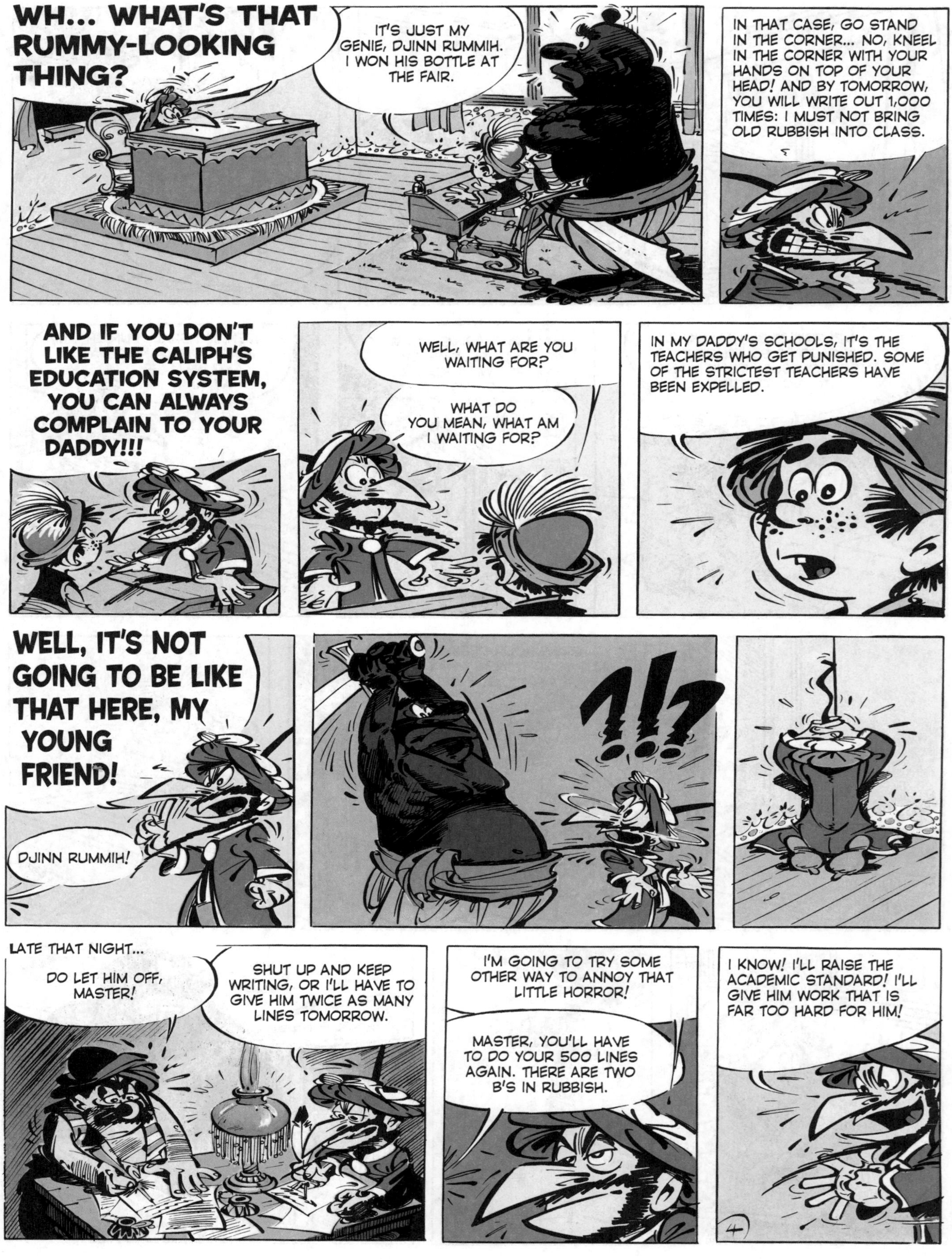
WH... WHAT'S THAT RUMMY-LOOKING THING?
IT'S JUST MY GENIE, DJINN RUMMIH. I WON HIS BOTTLE AT THE FAIR.
IN THAT CASE, GO STAND IN THE CORNER... NO, KNEEL IN THE CORNER WITH YOUR HANDS ON TOP OF YOUR HEAD! AND BY TOMORROW, YOU WILL WRITE OUT 1,000 TIMES: I MUST NOT BRING OLD RUBBISH INTO CLASS.
AND IF YOU DON'T LIKE THE CALIPH'S EDUCATION SYSTEM, YOU CAN ALWAYS COMPLAIN TO YOUR DADDY!!!
WELL, WHAT ARE YOU WAITING FOR?
WHAT DO YOU MEAN, WHAT AM I WAITING FOR?
IN MY DADDY'S SCHOOLS, IT'S THE TEACHERS WHO GET PUNISHED. SOME OF THE STRICTEST TEACHERS HAVE BEEN EXPELLED.
WELL, IT'S NOT GOING TO BE LIKE THAT HERE, MY YOUNG FRIEND!
DJINN RUMMIH!
?!?
LATE THAT NIGHT...
DO LET HIM OFF, MASTER!
SHUT UP AND KEEP WRITING, OR I'LL HAVE TO GIVE HIM TWICE AS MANY LINES TOMORROW.
I'M GOING TO TRY SOME OTHER WAY TO ANNOY THAT LITTLE HORROR!
MASTER, YOU'LL HAVE TO DO YOUR 500 LINES AGAIN. THERE ARE TWO B'S IN RUBBISH.
I KNOW! I'LL RAISE THE ACADEMIC STANDARD! I'LL GIVE HIM WORK THAT IS FAR TOO HARD FOR HIM!

NEXT DAY...

GET OUT YOUR EXERCISE BOOKS. WE'RE GOING TO HAVE AN ARITHMETIC EXAM.

BUT I HAVEN'T STUDIED FOR IT!

SILENCE IN CLASS! I AM GIVEN 225 MELONS, PLUS 4,376 MELONS, PLUS 5,204 MELONS, PLUS 643 MELONS, PLUS 708 MELONS. HOW MANY MELONS DO I GET IN ALL?

HAND IN YOUR ANSWER IN 30 SECONDS.

DJINN RUMMIH!

BONNG!

BING!

BONG!

OUCH!

EEK!

BONG!

THAT'S THE ANSWER. ALL YOU HAVE TO DO IS COUNT THE MELONS, BUT YOU CAN TRUST DJINN RUMMIH TO BE RIGHT. HE'S A MATHEMATICAL GENIUS.

BOOHOOHOO! I CAN'T COMPETE WITH A GENIUS GENIE!

THEN CONFISCATE THE GENIE.

CONFISCATION! YES, ALL SCHOOLBOYS HATE HAVING THEIR THINGS CONFISCATED!

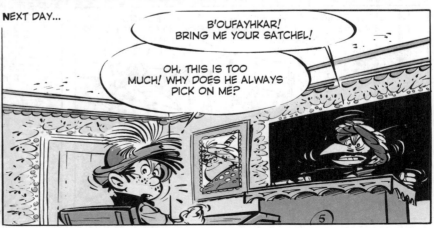

NEXT DAY...

B'OUFAYHKAR! BRING ME YOUR SATCHEL!

OH, THIS IS TOO MUCH! WHY DOES HE ALWAYS PICK ON ME?

5

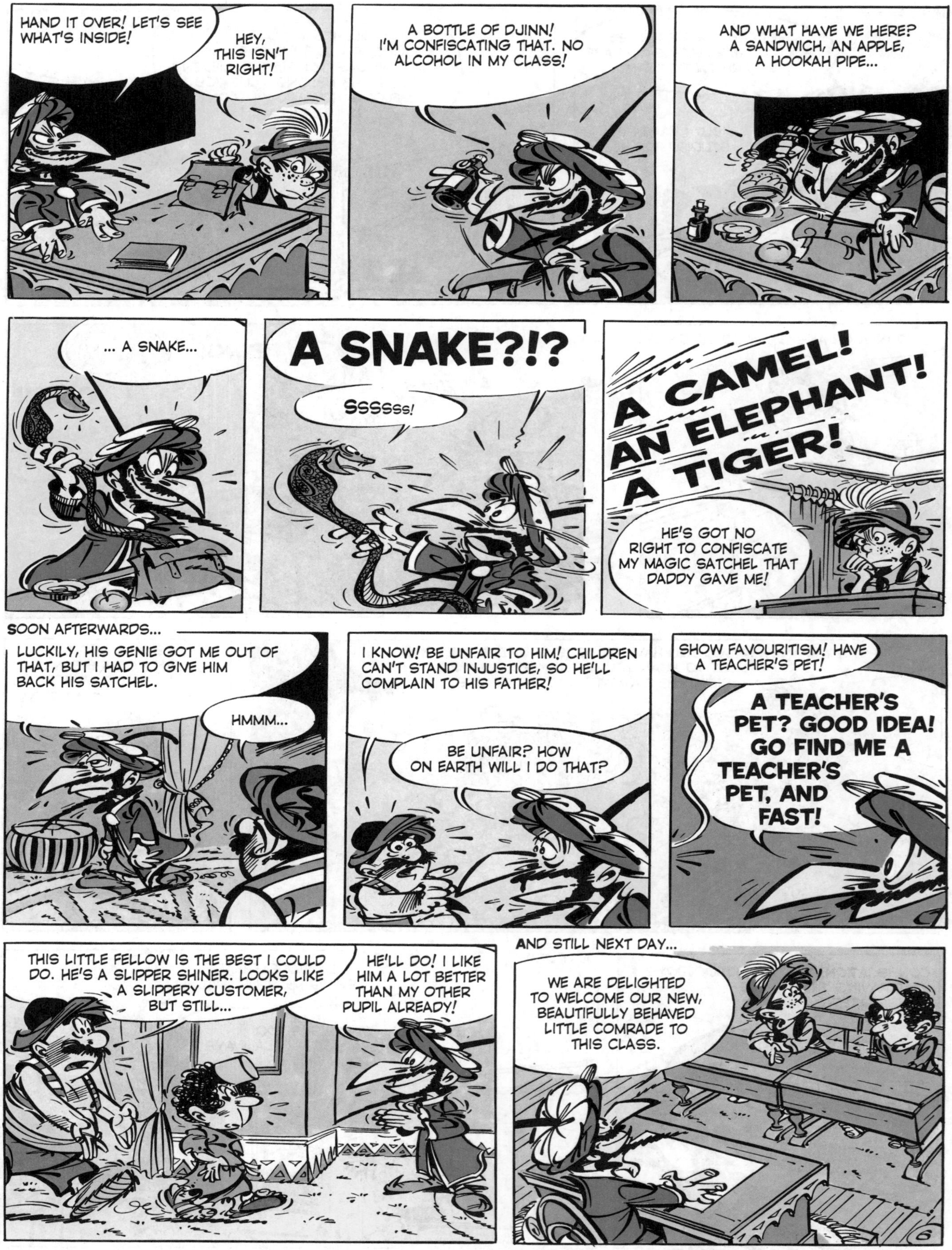
HAND IT OVER! LET'S SEE WHAT'S INSIDE!
HEY, THIS ISN'T RIGHT!
A BOTTLE OF DJINN! I'M CONFISCATING THAT. NO ALCOHOL IN MY CLASS!
AND WHAT HAVE WE HERE? A SANDWICH, AN APPLE, A HOOKAH PIPE...
... A SNAKE...
A SNAKE?!?
SSSSSS!
A CAMEL! AN ELEPHANT! A TIGER!
HE'S GOT NO RIGHT TO CONFISCATE MY MAGIC SATCHEL THAT DADDY GAVE ME!
SOON AFTERWARDS...
LUCKILY, HIS GENIE GOT ME OUT OF THAT, BUT I HAD TO GIVE HIM BACK HIS SATCHEL.
HMMM...
I KNOW! BE UNFAIR TO HIM! CHILDREN CAN'T STAND INJUSTICE, SO HE'LL COMPLAIN TO HIS FATHER!
BE UNFAIR? HOW ON EARTH WILL I DO THAT?
SHOW FAVOURITISM! HAVE A TEACHER'S PET!
A TEACHER'S PET? GOOD IDEA! GO FIND ME A TEACHER'S PET, AND FAST!
THIS LITTLE FELLOW IS THE BEST I COULD DO. HE'S A SLIPPER SHINER. LOOKS LIKE A SLIPPERY CUSTOMER, BUT STILL...
HE'LL DO! I LIKE HIM A LOT BETTER THAN MY OTHER PUPIL ALREADY!
AND STILL NEXT DAY...
WE ARE DELIGHTED TO WELCOME OUR NEW, BEAUTIFULLY BEHAVED LITTLE COMRADE TO THIS CLASS.

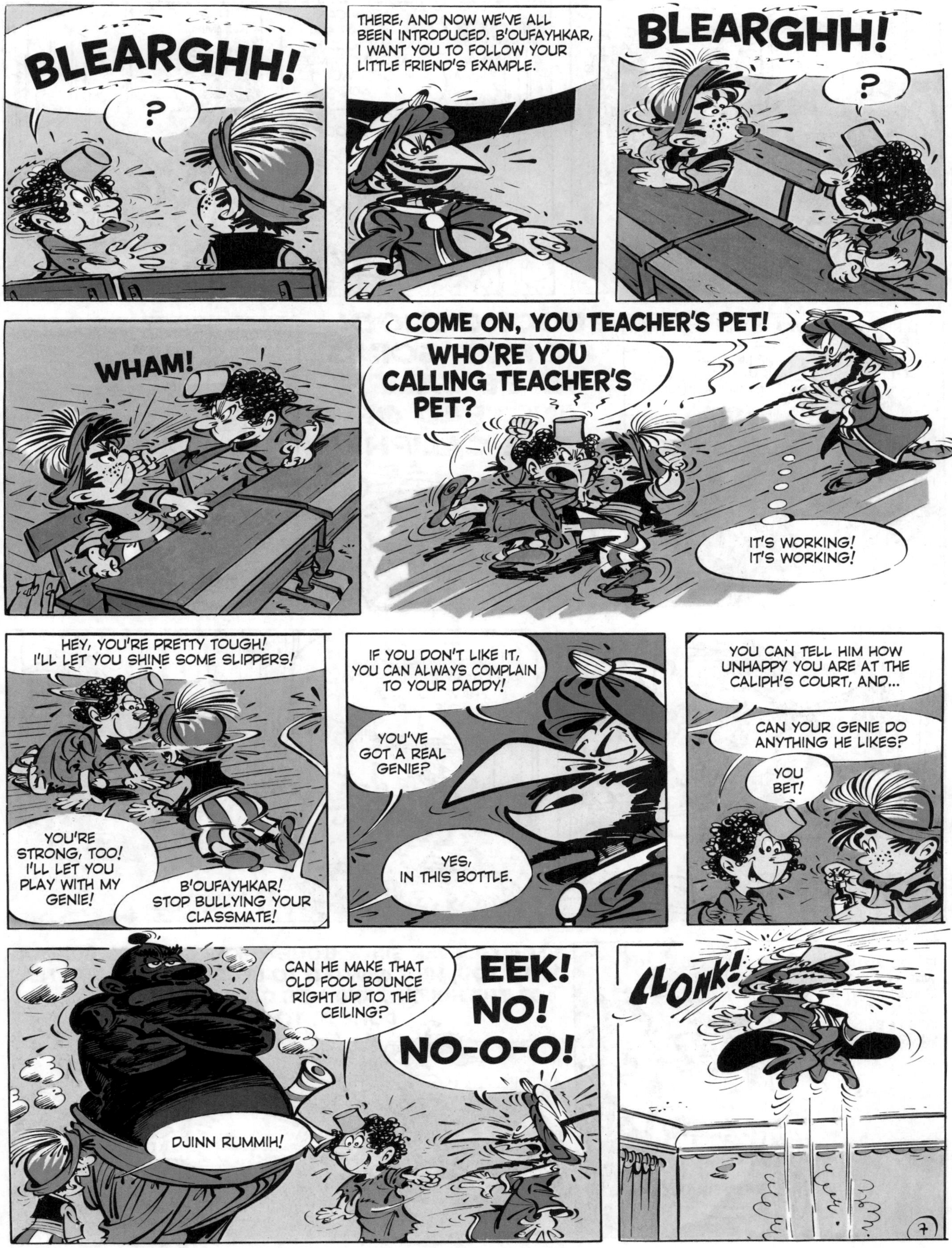
BLEARGHH!
?
THERE, AND NOW WE'VE ALL BEEN INTRODUCED. B'OUFAYHKAR, I WANT YOU TO FOLLOW YOUR LITTLE FRIEND'S EXAMPLE.
BLEARGHH!
?
WHAM!
COME ON, YOU TEACHER'S PET!
WHO'RE YOU CALLING TEACHER'S PET?
IT'S WORKING! IT'S WORKING!
HEY, YOU'RE PRETTY TOUGH! I'LL LET YOU SHINE SOME SLIPPERS!
YOU'RE STRONG, TOO! I'LL LET YOU PLAY WITH MY GENIE!
B'OUFAYHKAR! STOP BULLYING YOUR CLASSMATE!
IF YOU DON'T LIKE IT, YOU CAN ALWAYS COMPLAIN TO YOUR DADDY!
YOU'VE GOT A REAL GENIE?
YES, IN THIS BOTTLE.
YOU CAN TELL HIM HOW UNHAPPY YOU ARE AT THE CALIPH'S COURT, AND...
CAN YOUR GENIE DO ANYTHING HE LIKES?
YOU BET!
CAN HE MAKE THAT OLD FOOL BOUNCE RIGHT UP TO THE CEILING?
EEK! NO! NO-O-O!
DJINN RUMMIH!
CLONK!
7

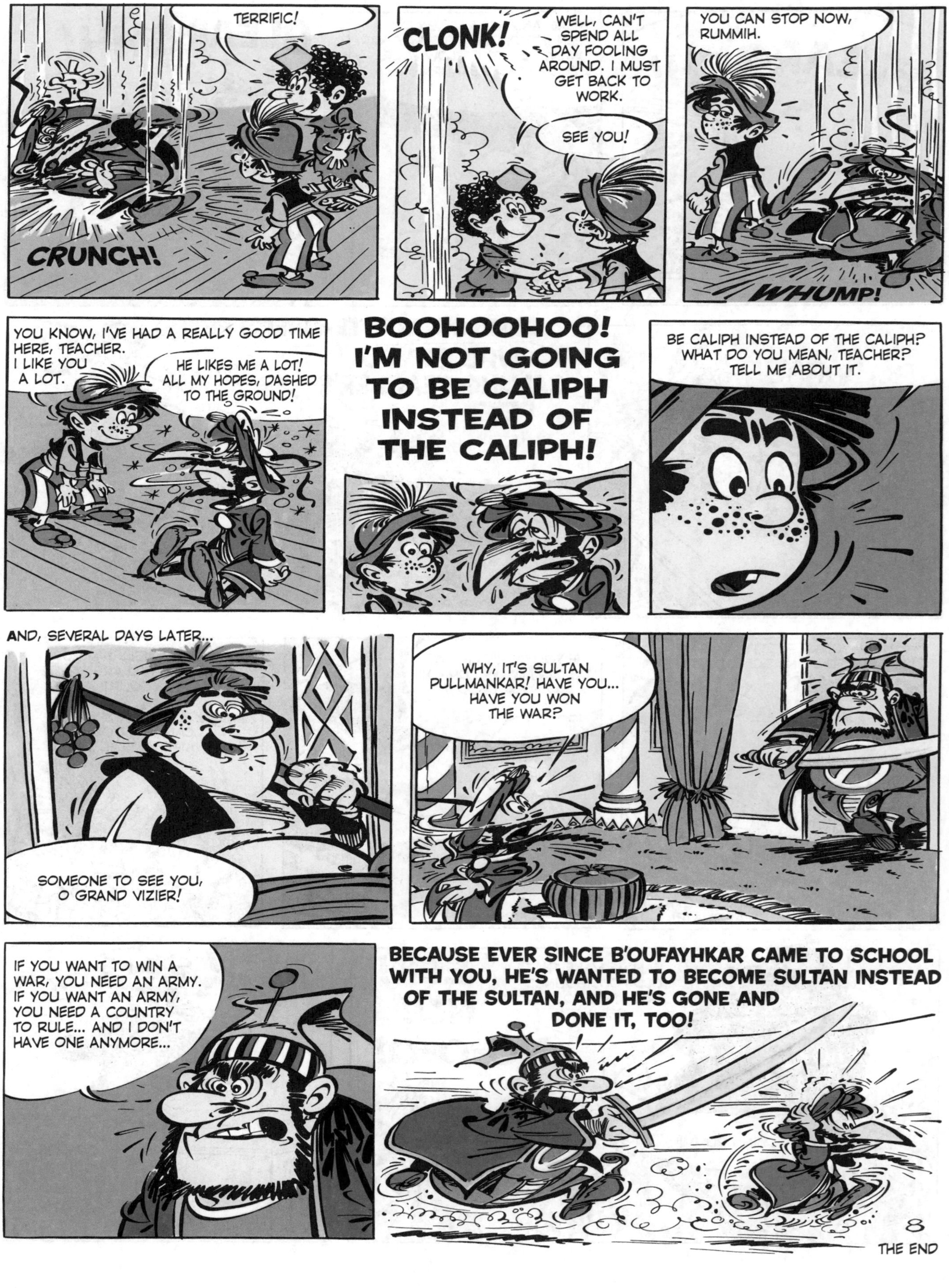
TERRIFIC!
CRUNCH!
CLONK!
WELL, CAN'T SPEND ALL DAY FOOLING AROUND. I MUST GET BACK TO WORK.
SEE YOU!
YOU CAN STOP NOW, RUMMIH.
WHUMP!
YOU KNOW, I'VE HAD A REALLY GOOD TIME HERE, TEACHER. I LIKE YOU A LOT.
HE LIKES ME A LOT! ALL MY HOPES, DASHED TO THE GROUND!
BOOHOOHOO! I'M NOT GOING TO BE CALIPH INSTEAD OF THE CALIPH!
BE CALIPH INSTEAD OF THE CALIPH? WHAT DO YOU MEAN, TEACHER? TELL ME ABOUT IT.
AND, SEVERAL DAYS LATER...
SOMEONE TO SEE YOU, O GRAND VIZIER!
WHY, IT'S SULTAN PULLMANKAR! HAVE YOU... HAVE YOU WON THE WAR?
IF YOU WANT TO WIN A WAR, YOU NEED AN ARMY. IF YOU WANT AN ARMY, YOU NEED A COUNTRY TO RULE... AND I DON'T HAVE ONE ANYMORE...
BECAUSE EVER SINCE B'OUFAYHKAR CAME TO SCHOOL WITH YOU, HE'S WANTED TO BECOME SULTAN INSTEAD OF THE SULTAN, AND HE'S GONE AND DONE IT, TOO!
8
THE END

# THE TARTAR'S TALISMAN

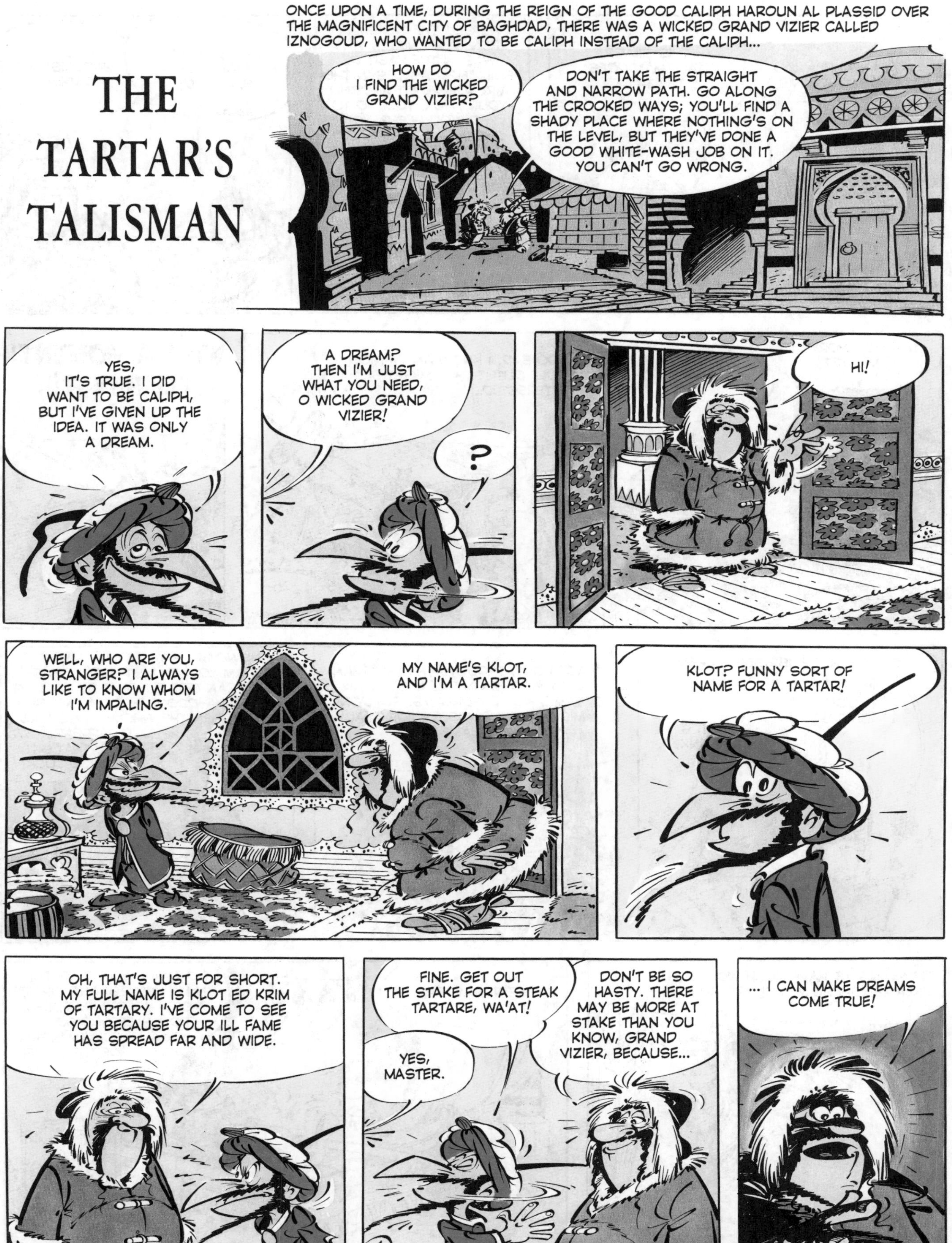
ONCE UPON A TIME, DURING THE REIGN OF THE GOOD CALIPH HAROUN AL PLASSID OVER THE MAGNIFICENT CITY OF BAGHDAD, THERE WAS A WICKED GRAND VIZIER CALLED IZNOGOUD, WHO WANTED TO BE CALIPH INSTEAD OF THE CALIPH...
HOW DO I FIND THE WICKED GRAND VIZIER?
DON'T TAKE THE STRAIGHT AND NARROW PATH. GO ALONG THE CROOKED WAYS; YOU'LL FIND A SHADY PLACE WHERE NOTHING'S ON THE LEVEL, BUT THEY'VE DONE A GOOD WHITE-WASH JOB ON IT. YOU CAN'T GO WRONG.
YES, IT'S TRUE. I DID WANT TO BE CALIPH, BUT I'VE GIVEN UP THE IDEA. IT WAS ONLY A DREAM.
A DREAM? THEN I'M JUST WHAT YOU NEED, O WICKED GRAND VIZIER!
?
HI!
WELL, WHO ARE YOU, STRANGER? I ALWAYS LIKE TO KNOW WHOM I'M IMPALING.
MY NAME'S KLOT, AND I'M A TARTAR.
KLOT? FUNNY SORT OF NAME FOR A TARTAR!
OH, THAT'S JUST FOR SHORT. MY FULL NAME IS KLOT ED KRIM OF TARTARY. I'VE COME TO SEE YOU BECAUSE YOUR ILL FAME HAS SPREAD FAR AND WIDE.
FINE. GET OUT THE STAKE FOR A STEAK TARTARE, WA'AT!
YES, MASTER.
DON'T BE SO HASTY. THERE MAY BE MORE AT STAKE THAN YOU KNOW, GRAND VIZIER, BECAUSE...
... I CAN MAKE DREAMS COME TRUE!

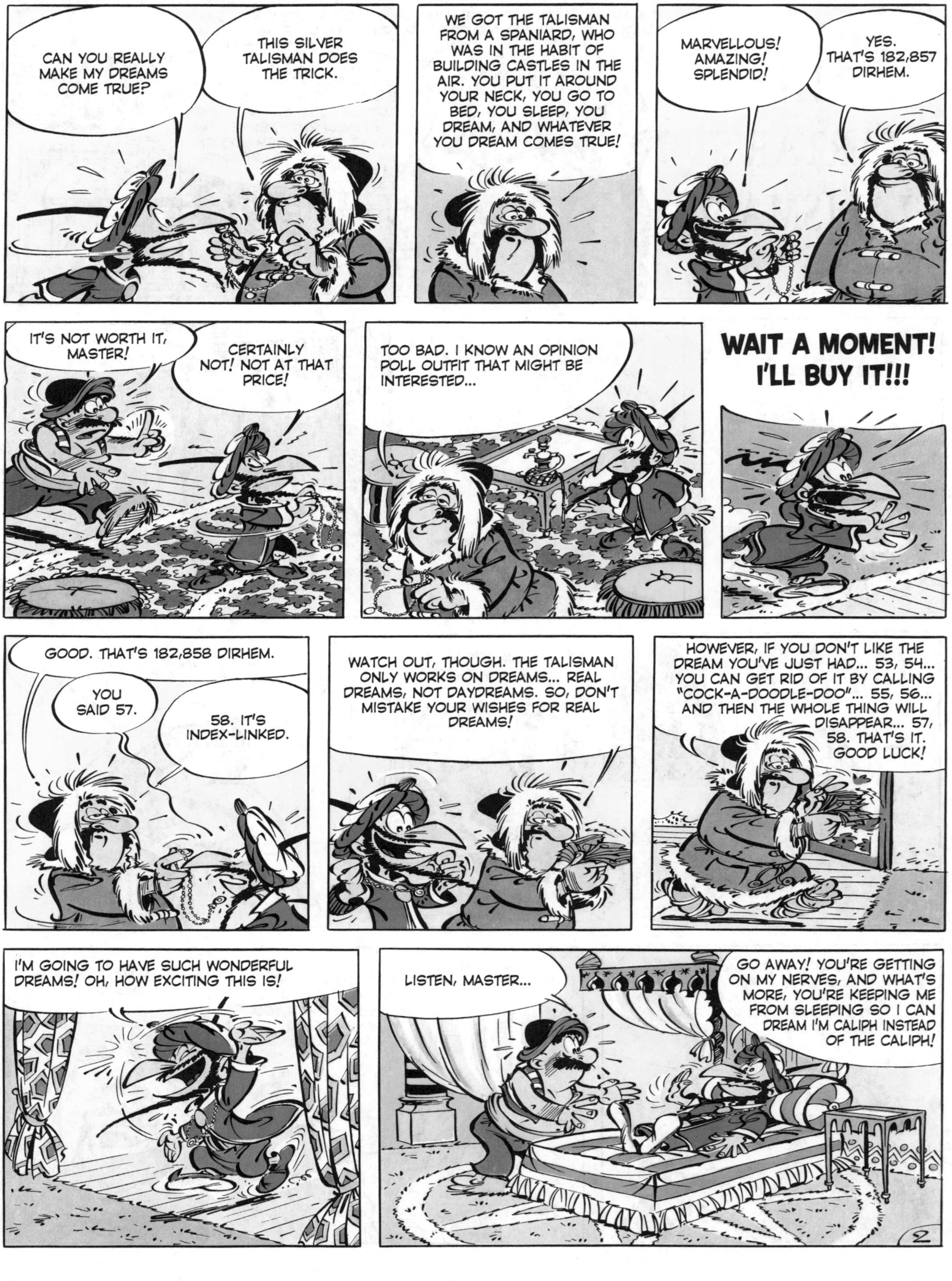
CAN YOU REALLY MAKE MY DREAMS COME TRUE?
THIS SILVER TALISMAN DOES THE TRICK.
WE GOT THE TALISMAN FROM A SPANIARD, WHO WAS IN THE HABIT OF BUILDING CASTLES IN THE AIR. YOU PUT IT AROUND YOUR NECK, YOU GO TO BED, YOU SLEEP, YOU DREAM, AND WHATEVER YOU DREAM COMES TRUE!
MARVELLOUS! AMAZING! SPLENDID!
YES. THAT'S 182,857 DIRHEM.
IT'S NOT WORTH IT, MASTER!
CERTAINLY NOT! NOT AT THAT PRICE!
TOO BAD. I KNOW AN OPINION POLL OUTFIT THAT MIGHT BE INTERESTED...
WAIT A MOMENT! I'LL BUY IT!!!
GOOD. THAT'S 182,858 DIRHEM.
YOU SAID 57.
58. IT'S INDEX-LINKED.
WATCH OUT, THOUGH. THE TALISMAN ONLY WORKS ON DREAMS... REAL DREAMS, NOT DAYDREAMS. SO, DON'T MISTAKE YOUR WISHES FOR REAL DREAMS!
HOWEVER, IF YOU DON'T LIKE THE DREAM YOU'VE JUST HAD... 53, 54... YOU CAN GET RID OF IT BY CALLING "COCK-A-DOODLE-DOO"... 55, 56... AND THEN THE WHOLE THING WILL DISAPPEAR... 57, 58. THAT'S IT. GOOD LUCK!
I'M GOING TO HAVE SUCH WONDERFUL DREAMS! OH, HOW EXCITING THIS IS!
LISTEN, MASTER...
GO AWAY! YOU'RE GETTING ON MY NERVES, AND WHAT'S MORE, YOU'RE KEEPING ME FROM SLEEPING SO I CAN DREAM I'M CALIPH INSTEAD OF THE CALIPH!
2

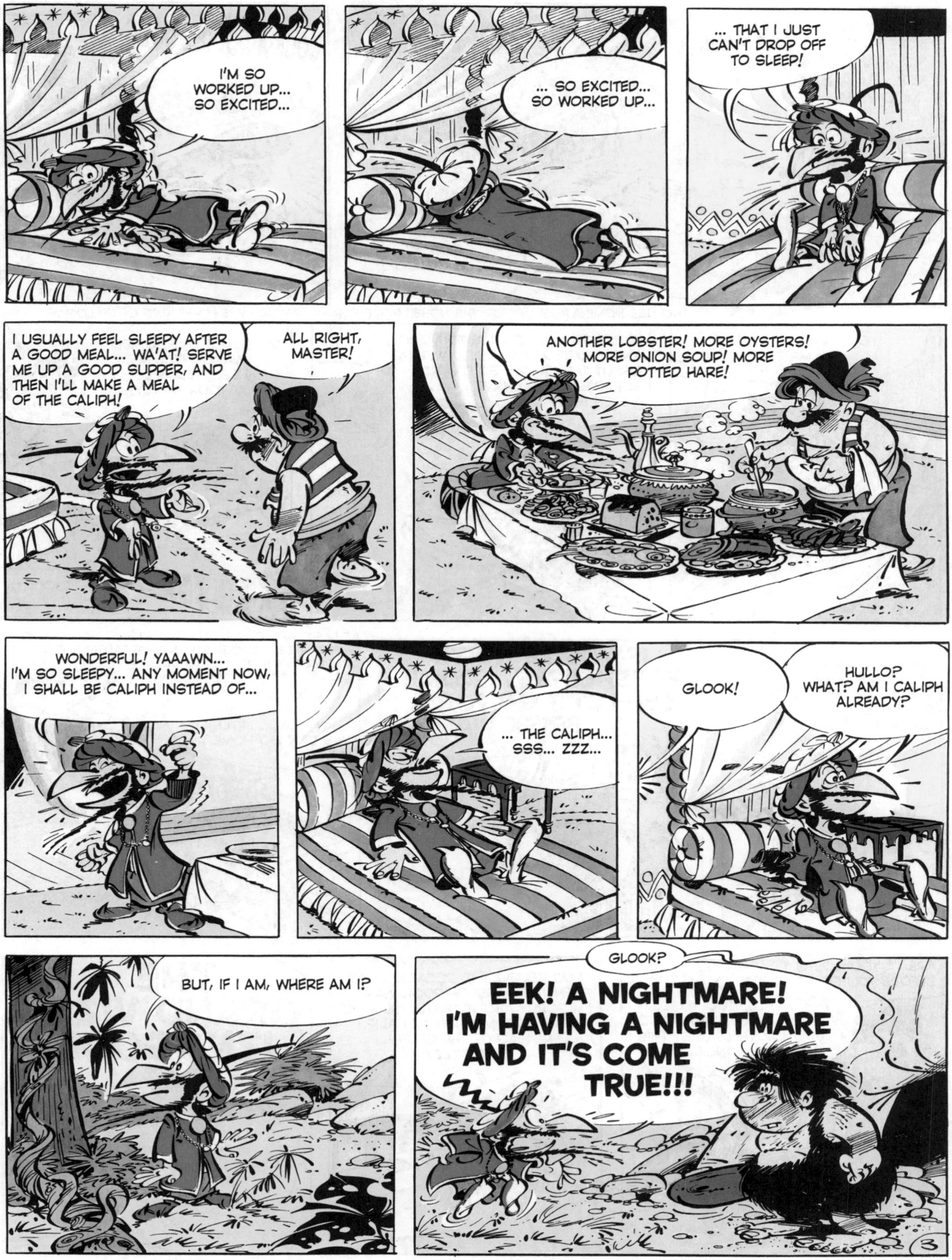
I'M SO WORKED UP... SO EXCITED...
... SO EXCITED... SO WORKED UP...
... THAT I JUST CAN'T DROP OFF TO SLEEP!
I USUALLY FEEL SLEEPY AFTER A GOOD MEAL... WA'AT! SERVE ME UP A GOOD SUPPER, AND THEN I'LL MAKE A MEAL OF THE CALIPH!
ALL RIGHT, MASTER!
ANOTHER LOBSTER! MORE OYSTERS! MORE ONION SOUP! MORE POTTED HARE!
WONDERFUL! YAAAWN... I'M SO SLEEPY... ANY MOMENT NOW, I SHALL BE CALIPH INSTEAD OF...
... THE CALIPH... SSS... ZZZ...
GLOOK!
HULLO? WHAT? AM I CALIPH ALREADY?
BUT, IF I AM, WHERE AM I?
GLOOK?
EEK! A NIGHTMARE! I'M HAVING A NIGHTMARE AND IT'S COME TRUE!!!

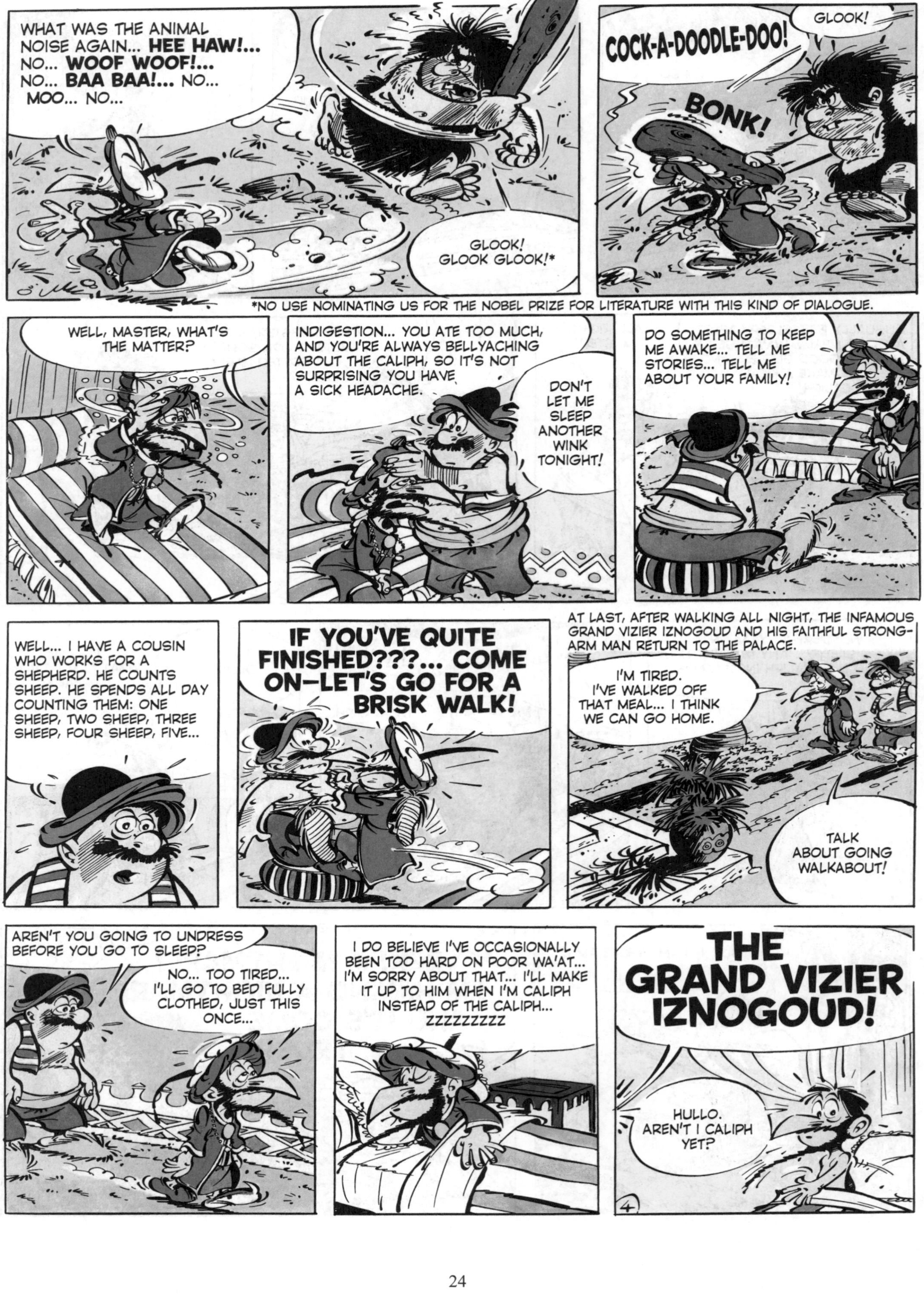
WHAT WAS THE ANIMAL NOISE AGAIN... HEE HAW!... NO... WOOF WOOF!... NO... BAA BAA!... NO... MOO... NO...
GLOOK! GLOOK GLOOK!*
COCK-A-DOODLE-DOO!
GLOOK!
BONK!
*NO USE NOMINATING US FOR THE NOBEL PRIZE FOR LITERATURE WITH THIS KIND OF DIALOGUE.
WELL, MASTER, WHAT'S THE MATTER?
INDIGESTION... YOU ATE TOO MUCH, AND YOU'RE ALWAYS BELLYACHING ABOUT THE CALIPH, SO IT'S NOT SURPRISING YOU HAVE A SICK HEADACHE.
DON'T LET ME SLEEP ANOTHER WINK TONIGHT!
DO SOMETHING TO KEEP ME AWAKE... TELL ME STORIES... TELL ME ABOUT YOUR FAMILY!
WELL... I HAVE A COUSIN WHO WORKS FOR A SHEPHERD. HE COUNTS SHEEP. HE SPENDS ALL DAY COUNTING THEM: ONE SHEEP, TWO SHEEP, THREE SHEEP, FOUR SHEEP, FIVE...
IF YOU'VE QUITE FINISHED???... COME ON—LET'S GO FOR A BRISK WALK!
AT LAST, AFTER WALKING ALL NIGHT, THE INFAMOUS GRAND VIZIER IZNOGOUD AND HIS FAITHFUL STRONG-ARM MAN RETURN TO THE PALACE.
I'M TIRED. I'VE WALKED OFF THAT MEAL... I THINK WE CAN GO HOME.
TALK ABOUT GOING WALKABOUT!
AREN'T YOU GOING TO UNDRESS BEFORE YOU GO TO SLEEP?
NO... TOO TIRED... I'LL GO TO BED FULLY CLOTHED, JUST THIS ONCE...
I DO BELIEVE I'VE OCCASIONALLY BEEN TOO HARD ON POOR WA'AT... I'M SORRY ABOUT THAT... I'LL MAKE IT UP TO HIM WHEN I'M CALIPH INSTEAD OF THE CALIPH... ZZZZZZZZZ
THE GRAND VIZIER IZNOGOUD!
HULLO. AREN'T I CALIPH YET?

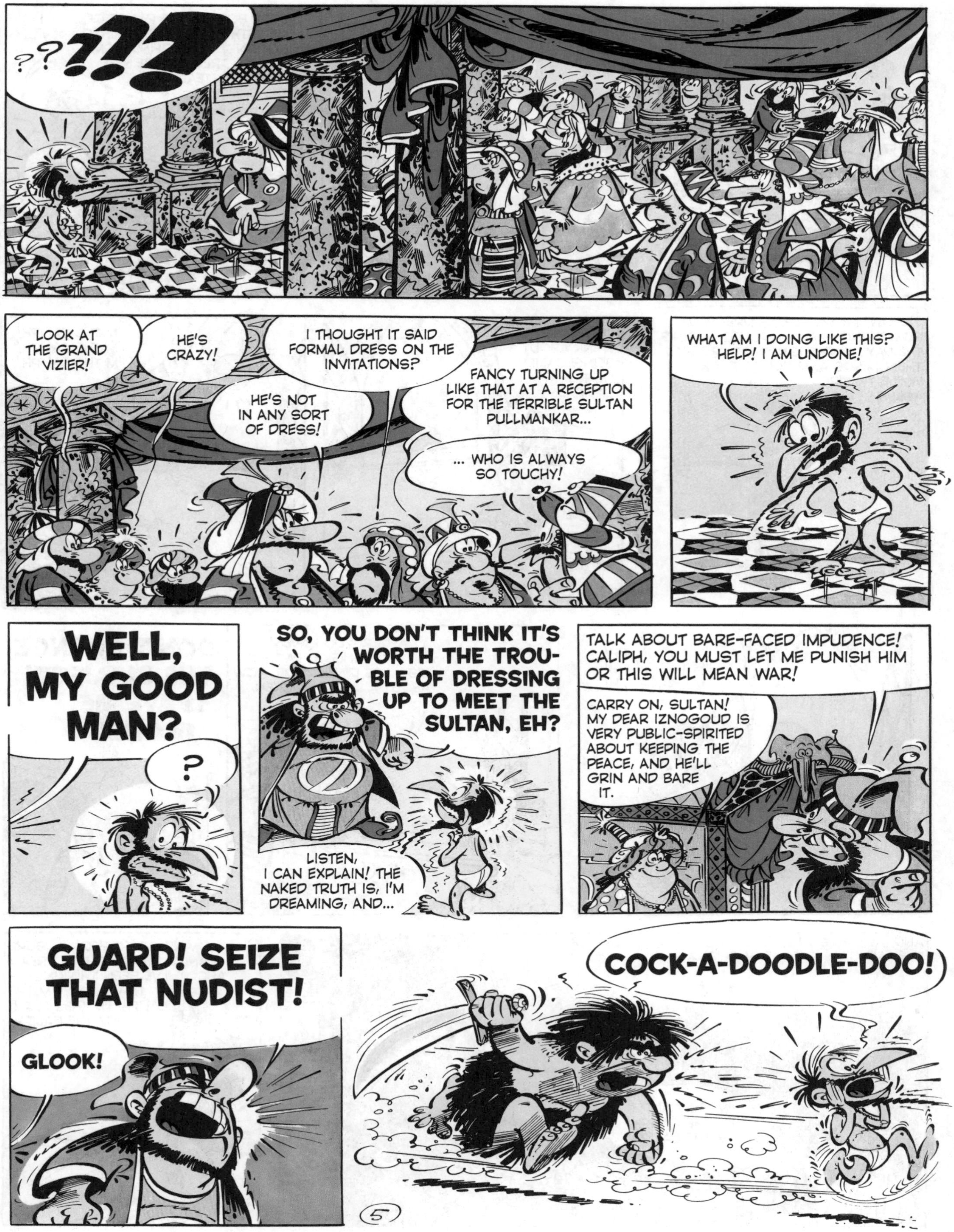

??
LOOK AT THE GRAND VIZIER!
HE'S CRAZY!
I THOUGHT IT SAID FORMAL DRESS ON THE INVITATIONS?
HE'S NOT IN ANY SORT OF DRESS!
FANCY TURNING UP LIKE THAT AT A RECEPTION FOR THE TERRIBLE SULTAN PULLMANKAR...
... WHO IS ALWAYS SO TOUCHY!
WHAT AM I DOING LIKE THIS? HELP! I AM UNDONE!
WELL, MY GOOD MAN?
?
SO, YOU DON'T THINK IT'S WORTH THE TROUBLE OF DRESSING UP TO MEET THE SULTAN, EH?
LISTEN, I CAN EXPLAIN! THE NAKED TRUTH IS, I'M DREAMING, AND...
TALK ABOUT BARE-FACED IMPUDENCE! CALIPH, YOU MUST LET ME PUNISH HIM OR THIS WILL MEAN WAR!
CARRY ON, SULTAN! MY DEAR IZNOGOUD IS VERY PUBLIC-SPIRITED ABOUT KEEPING THE PEACE, AND HE'LL GRIN AND BARE IT.
GUARD! SEIZE THAT NUDIST!
GLOOK!
COCK-A-DOODLE-DOO!
5

WELL, MASTER? ANOTHER NIGHTMARE?

I... I WAS PRACTICALLY NAKED, AND...

NAKED? OH, YES, A VERY COMMON DREAM. IT CAN OFTEN BE ASCRIBED TO A GUILT COMPLEX, WHICH...

STOP BORING THE PANTS OFF ME WITH YOUR BIRD-BRAINED NOTIONS! I MUST FIND SOME WAY TO DREAM OF BEING CALIPH INSTEAD OF THE CALIPH!

I KNOW! PEOPLE OFTEN DREAM OF SOMETHING THAT HAPPENED DURING THE DAY... A THOUGHT THAT CROSSED THEIR MINDS AND COMES BACK WHILE THEY'RE ASLEEP...

I'M GOING TO THINK ABOUT BEING CALIPH... I'M THE CALIPH...

I'M THE CALIPH! I'M THE CALIPH! I'M THE CALIPH!

I'M THE CALIPH! I'M THE CALIPH! I'M THE CALIPH!

I'M THE...

MASTER, YOU HAVEN'T HAD ANYTHING TO EAT FOR AGES... IT'S DINNERTIME. HOW ABOUT A LITTLE CHICKEN, MAYBE?

# DON'T CHANGE THE SUBJECT! LEAVE ME ALONE!

ALL RIGHT.

AND, AS THE SUN SETS BEHIND THE ROOFTOPS OF THE FAIRYTALE CITY OF BAGHDAD...

I'M THE CALIPH! I'M THE CALIPH! I'M THE CALIPH!

AND SO TO BED! I'M SURE I KNOW WHAT I SHALL DREAM ABOUT. I'VE BEEN THINKING OF IT ALL DAY! I'M THE CALIPH! I'M THE CALIPH! I'M THE CALIPH!

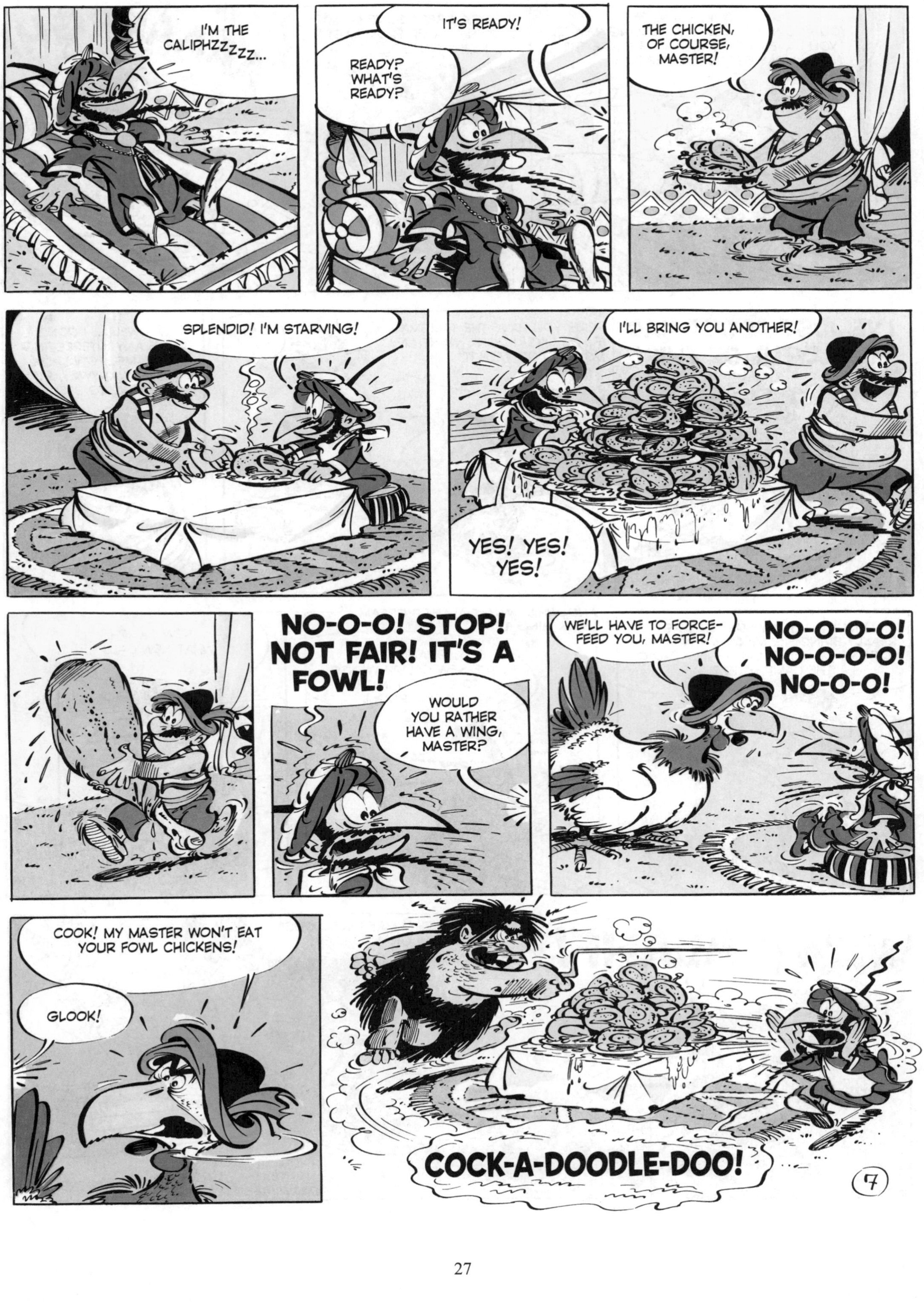
I'M THE CALIPHZZZZZZ...
IT'S READY!
READY? WHAT'S READY?
THE CHICKEN, OF COURSE, MASTER!
SPLENDID! I'M STARVING!
I'LL BRING YOU ANOTHER!
YES! YES! YES!
NO-O-O! STOP! NOT FAIR! IT'S A FOWL!
WOULD YOU RATHER HAVE A WING, MASTER?
WE'LL HAVE TO FORCE-FEED YOU, MASTER!
NO-O-O-O! NO-O-O-O! NO-O-O!
COOK! MY MASTER WON'T EAT YOUR FOWL CHICKENS!
GLOOK!
COCK-A-DOODLE-DOO!
7

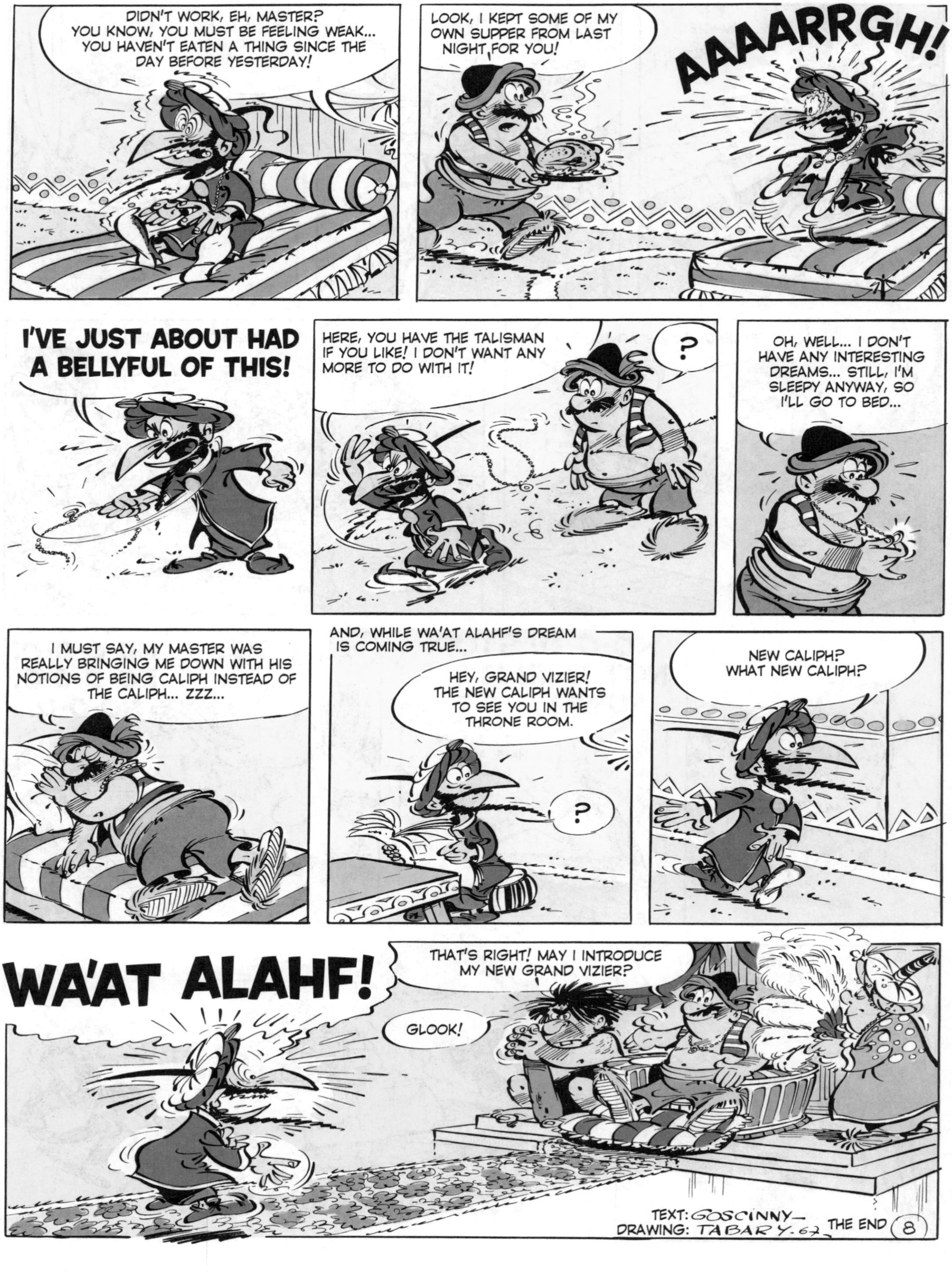

DIDN'T WORK, EH, MASTER? YOU KNOW, YOU MUST BE FEELING WEAK... YOU HAVEN'T EATEN A THING SINCE THE DAY BEFORE YESTERDAY!
LOOK, I KEPT SOME OF MY OWN SUPPER FROM LAST NIGHT FOR YOU!
AAAARRGH!
I'VE JUST ABOUT HAD A BELLYFUL OF THIS!
HERE, YOU HAVE THE TALISMAN IF YOU LIKE! I DON'T WANT ANY MORE TO DO WITH IT!
?
OH, WELL... I DON'T HAVE ANY INTERESTING DREAMS... STILL, I'M SLEEPY ANYWAY, SO I'LL GO TO BED...
I MUST SAY, MY MASTER WAS REALLY BRINGING ME DOWN WITH HIS NOTIONS OF BEING CALIPH INSTEAD OF THE CALIPH... ZZZ...
AND, WHILE WA'AT ALAHF'S DREAM IS COMING TRUE...
HEY, GRAND VIZIER! THE NEW CALIPH WANTS TO SEE YOU IN THE THRONE ROOM.
?
NEW CALIPH? WHAT NEW CALIPH?
WA'AT ALAHF!
THAT'S RIGHT! MAY I INTRODUCE MY NEW GRAND VIZIER?
GLOOK!
TEXT: GOSCINNY
DRAWING: TABARY.67
THE END
8

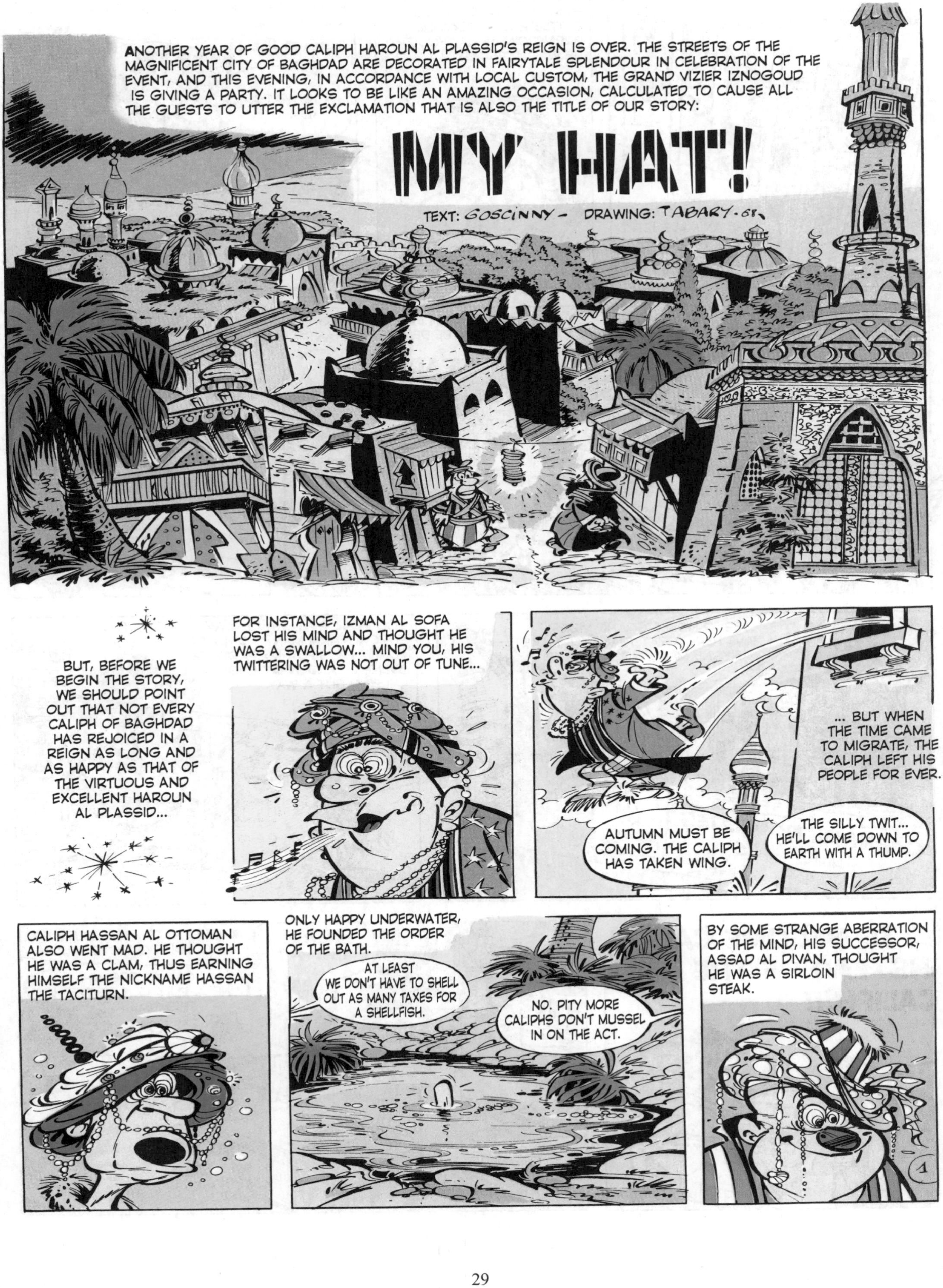

ANOTHER YEAR OF GOOD CALIPH HAROUN AL PLASSID'S REIGN IS OVER. THE STREETS OF THE MAGNIFICENT CITY OF BAGHDAD ARE DECORATED IN FAIRYTALE SPLENDOUR IN CELEBRATION OF THE EVENT, AND THIS EVENING, IN ACCORDANCE WITH LOCAL CUSTOM, THE GRAND VIZIER IZNOGOUD IS GIVING A PARTY. IT LOOKS TO BE LIKE AN AMAZING OCCASION, CALCULATED TO CAUSE ALL THE GUESTS TO UTTER THE EXCLAMATION THAT IS ALSO THE TITLE OF OUR STORY:
MY HAT!
TEXT: GOSCINNY - DRAWING: TABARY - 68
BUT, BEFORE WE BEGIN THE STORY, WE SHOULD POINT OUT THAT NOT EVERY CALIPH OF BAGHDAD HAS REJOICED IN A REIGN AS LONG AND AS HAPPY AS THAT OF THE VIRTUOUS AND EXCELLENT HAROUN AL PLASSID...
FOR INSTANCE, IZMAN AL SOFA LOST HIS MIND AND THOUGHT HE WAS A SWALLOW... MIND YOU, HIS TWITTERING WAS NOT OUT OF TUNE...
... BUT WHEN THE TIME CAME TO MIGRATE, THE CALIPH LEFT HIS PEOPLE FOR EVER.
AUTUMN MUST BE COMING. THE CALIPH HAS TAKEN WING.
THE SILLY TWIT... HE'LL COME DOWN TO EARTH WITH A THUMP.
CALIPH HASSAN AL OTTOMAN ALSO WENT MAD. HE THOUGHT HE WAS A CLAM, THUS EARNING HIMSELF THE NICKNAME HASSAN THE TACITURN.
ONLY HAPPY UNDERWATER, HE FOUNDED THE ORDER OF THE BATH.
AT LEAST WE DON'T HAVE TO SHELL OUT AS MANY TAXES FOR A SHELLFISH.
NO. PITY MORE CALIPHS DON'T MUSSEL IN ON THE ACT.
BY SOME STRANGE ABERRATION OF THE MIND, HIS SUCCESSOR, ASSAD AL DIVAN, THOUGHT HE WAS A SIRLOIN STEAK.
1

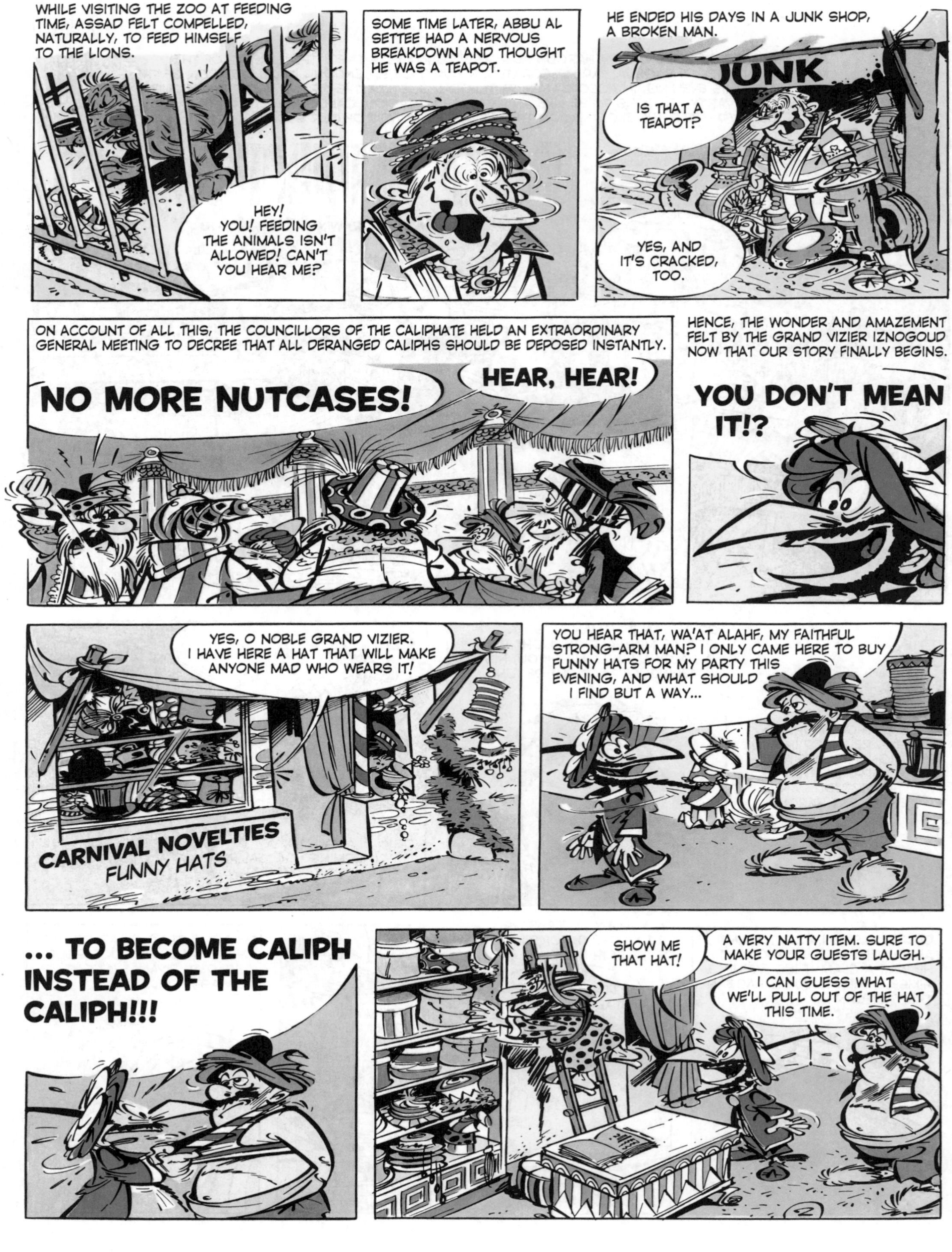
WHILE VISITING THE ZOO AT FEEDING TIME, ASSAD FELT COMPELLED, NATURALLY, TO FEED HIMSELF TO THE LIONS.
HEY! YOU! FEEDING THE ANIMALS ISN'T ALLOWED! CAN'T YOU HEAR ME?
SOME TIME LATER, ABBU AL SETTEE HAD A NERVOUS BREAKDOWN AND THOUGHT HE WAS A TEAPOT.
HE ENDED HIS DAYS IN A JUNK SHOP, A BROKEN MAN.
JUNK
IS THAT A TEAPOT?
YES, AND IT'S CRACKED, TOO.
ON ACCOUNT OF ALL THIS, THE COUNCILLORS OF THE CALIPHATE HELD AN EXTRAORDINARY GENERAL MEETING TO DECREE THAT ALL DERANGED CALIPHS SHOULD BE DEPOSED INSTANTLY.
NO MORE NUTCASES!
HEAR, HEAR!
HENCE, THE WONDER AND AMAZEMENT FELT BY THE GRAND VIZIER IZNOGOUD NOW THAT OUR STORY FINALLY BEGINS.
YOU DON'T MEAN IT!?
YES, O NOBLE GRAND VIZIER. I HAVE HERE A HAT THAT WILL MAKE ANYONE MAD WHO WEARS IT!
CARNIVAL NOVELTIES
FUNNY HATS
YOU HEAR THAT, WA'AT ALAHF, MY FAITHFUL STRONG-ARM MAN? I ONLY CAME HERE TO BUY FUNNY HATS FOR MY PARTY THIS EVENING, AND WHAT SHOULD I FIND BUT A WAY...
... TO BECOME CALIPH INSTEAD OF THE CALIPH!!!
SHOW ME THAT HAT!
A VERY NATTY ITEM. SURE TO MAKE YOUR GUESTS LAUGH.
I CAN GUESS WHAT WE'LL PULL OUT OF THE HAT THIS TIME.

HERE YOU ARE. ANYONE WHO PUTS THIS HAT ON GOES PERMANENTLY MAD. IT WILL BE A LOAD OF LAUGHS. YOUR GUESTS WILL BE CRAZY ABOUT IT!

IF YOU WANT MY OPINION, MASTER, THAT SHOPKEEPER IS TALKING THROUGH HIS HAT. HE'S MAD AS A HATTER!

IT WOULD REALLY SUIT YOU. WANT TO TRY IT ON?

WAIT A MINUTE.

SO, YOU DON'T BELIEVE IN IT?

FLYING CARPETS, YES. MAGIC LAMPS WITH GENIES IN THEM, YES. BUT, HATS THAT MAKE YOU CRAZY... NO, THAT'S INSANE!

THEN YOU DON'T MIND TRYING IT ON?

ANYTHING TO OBLIGE...

WHAT'S HAPPENED TO HIM?

HE THINKS HE'S SOMETHING OR OTHER... YOU MAY FIND OUT WHAT SOMEDAY.

OKAY, I'LL TAKE IT! YOU CAN DELIVER IT TO THE PALACE!

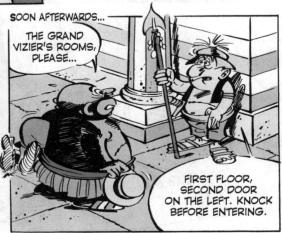

SOON AFTERWARDS...

THE GRAND VIZIER'S ROOMS, PLEASE...

FIRST FLOOR, SECOND DOOR ON THE LEFT. KNOCK BEFORE ENTERING.

COME IN!

KLUNK
KLUNK
KLUNK

3

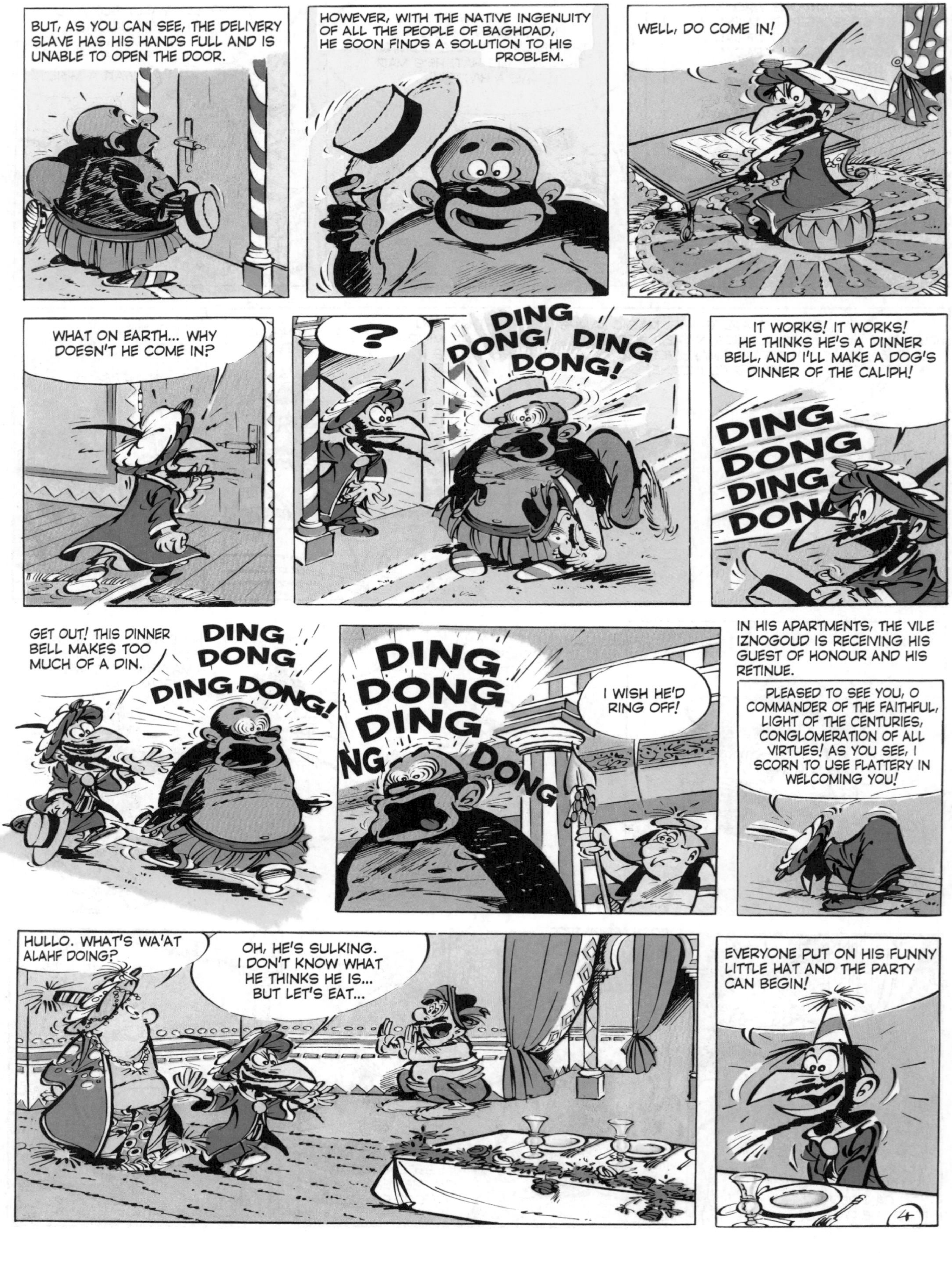

BUT, AS YOU CAN SEE, THE DELIVERY SLAVE HAS HIS HANDS FULL AND IS UNABLE TO OPEN THE DOOR.
HOWEVER, WITH THE NATIVE INGENUITY OF ALL THE PEOPLE OF BAGHDAD, HE SOON FINDS A SOLUTION TO HIS PROBLEM.
WELL, DO COME IN!
WHAT ON EARTH... WHY DOESN'T HE COME IN?
?
DING DONG DING DONG!
IT WORKS! IT WORKS! HE THINKS HE'S A DINNER BELL, AND I'LL MAKE A DOG'S DINNER OF THE CALIPH!
DING DONG DING DON
GET OUT! THIS DINNER BELL MAKES TOO MUCH OF A DIN.
DING DONG DING DONG!
DING DONG DING NG DONG
I WISH HE'D RING OFF!
IN HIS APARTMENTS, THE VILE IZNOGOUD IS RECEIVING HIS GUEST OF HONOUR AND HIS RETINUE.
PLEASED TO SEE YOU, O COMMANDER OF THE FAITHFUL, LIGHT OF THE CENTURIES, CONGLOMERATION OF ALL VIRTUES! AS YOU SEE, I SCORN TO USE FLATTERY IN WELCOMING YOU!
HULLO. WHAT'S WA'AT ALAHF DOING?
OH, HE'S SULKING. I DON'T KNOW WHAT HE THINKS HE IS... BUT LET'S EAT...
EVERYONE PUT ON HIS FUNNY LITTLE HAT AND THE PARTY CAN BEGIN!
4

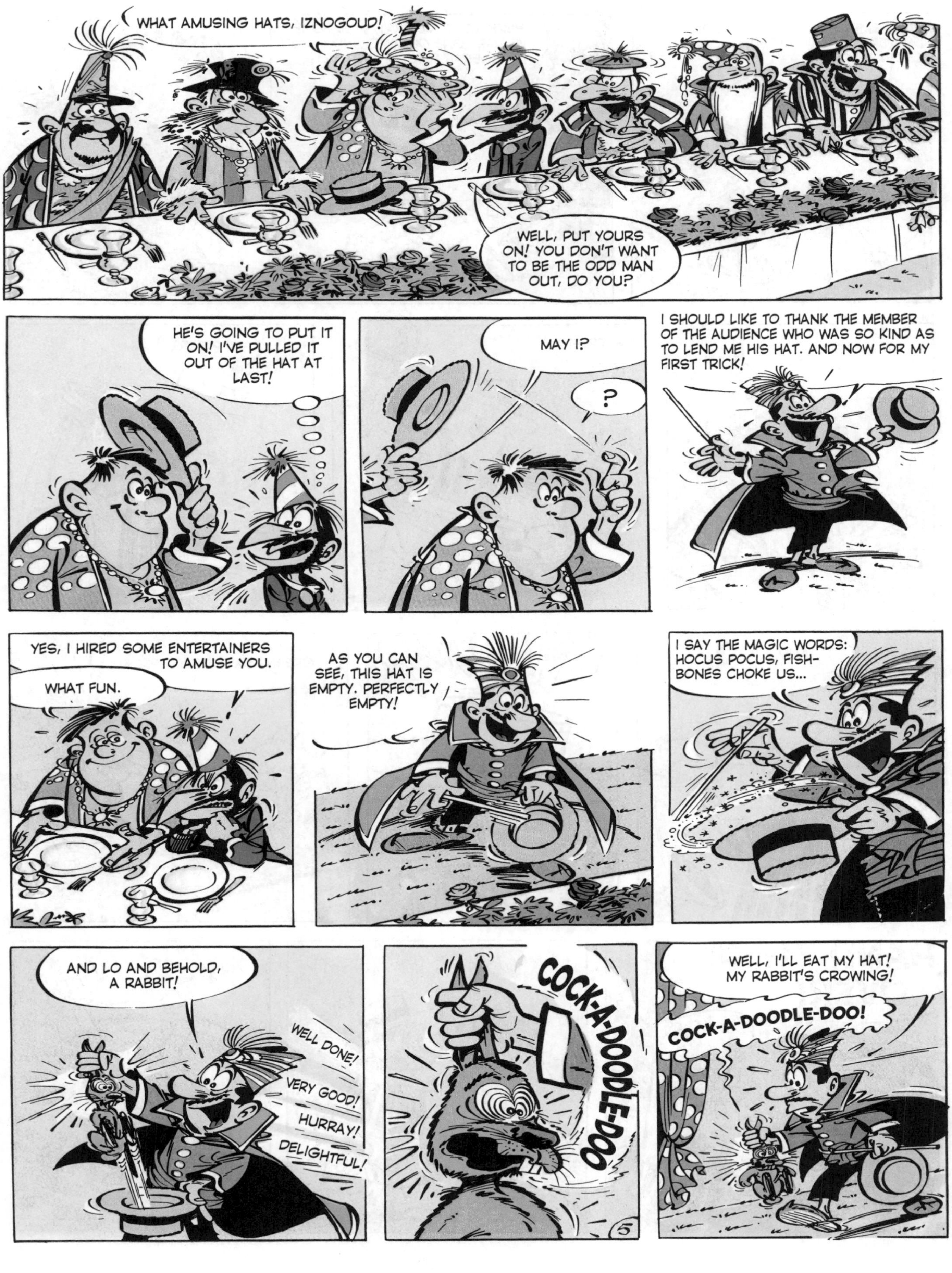
WHAT AMUSING HATS, IZNOGOUD!
WELL, PUT YOURS ON! YOU DON'T WANT TO BE THE ODD MAN OUT, DO YOU?
HE'S GOING TO PUT IT ON! I'VE PULLED IT OUT OF THE HAT AT LAST!
MAY I?
?
I SHOULD LIKE TO THANK THE MEMBER OF THE AUDIENCE WHO WAS SO KIND AS TO LEND ME HIS HAT. AND NOW FOR MY FIRST TRICK!
YES, I HIRED SOME ENTERTAINERS TO AMUSE YOU.
WHAT FUN.
AS YOU CAN SEE, THIS HAT IS EMPTY. PERFECTLY EMPTY!
I SAY THE MAGIC WORDS: HOCUS POCUS, FISH-BONES CHOKE US...
AND LO AND BEHOLD, A RABBIT!
WELL DONE!
VERY GOOD!
HURRAY!
DELIGHTFUL!
COCK-A-DOODLE-DOO
WELL, I'LL EAT MY HAT! MY RABBIT'S CROWING!
COCK-A-DOODLE-DOO!

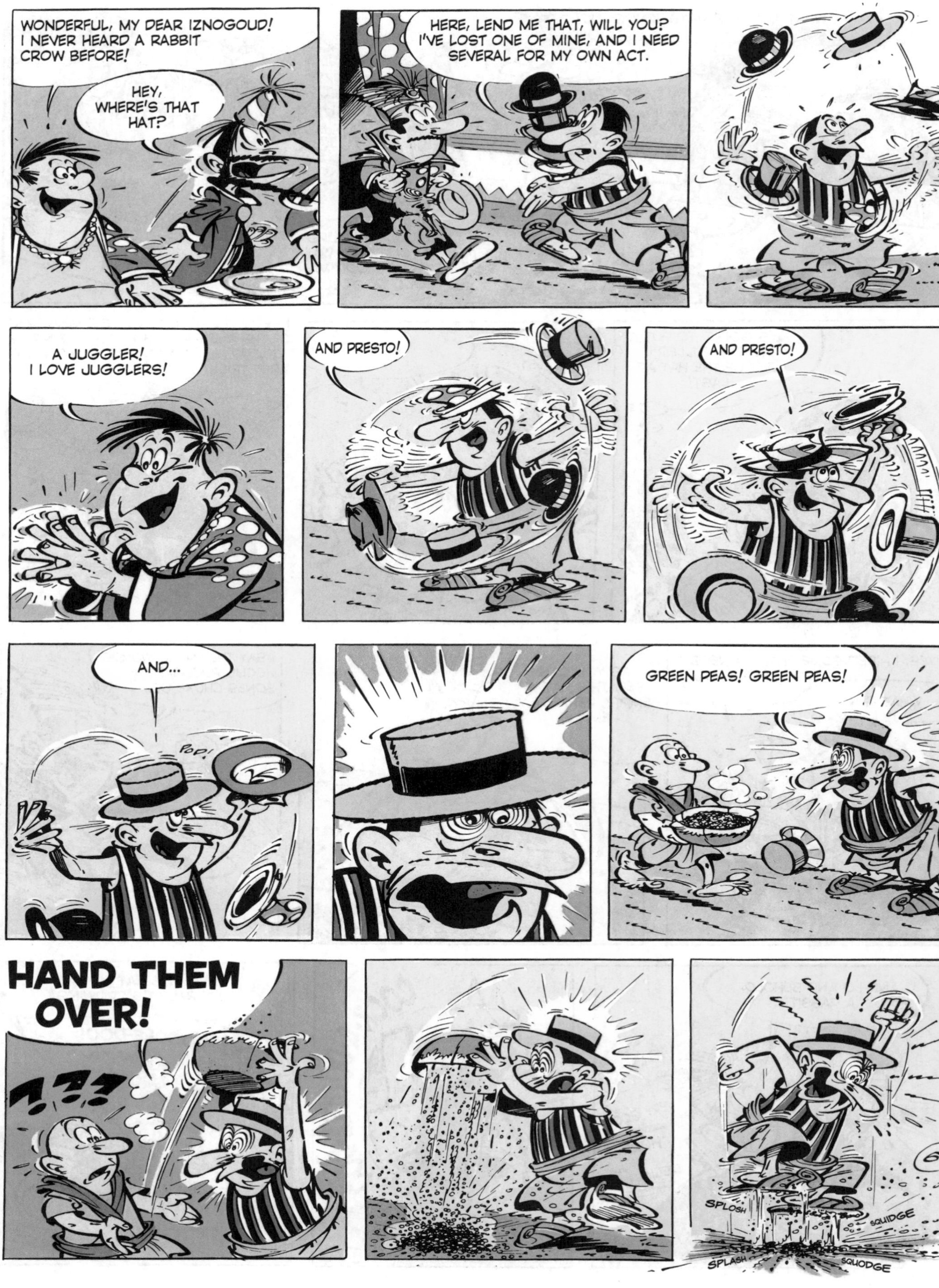
WONDERFUL, MY DEAR IZNOGOUD! I NEVER HEARD A RABBIT CROW BEFORE!
HEY, WHERE'S THAT HAT?
HERE, LEND ME THAT, WILL YOU? I'VE LOST ONE OF MINE, AND I NEED SEVERAL FOR MY OWN ACT.
A JUGGLER! I LOVE JUGGLERS!
AND PRESTO!
AND PRESTO!
AND...
POP!
GREEN PEAS! GREEN PEAS!
HAND THEM OVER!
?!??
SPLASH
SQUIDGE
SPLASH
SQUODGE

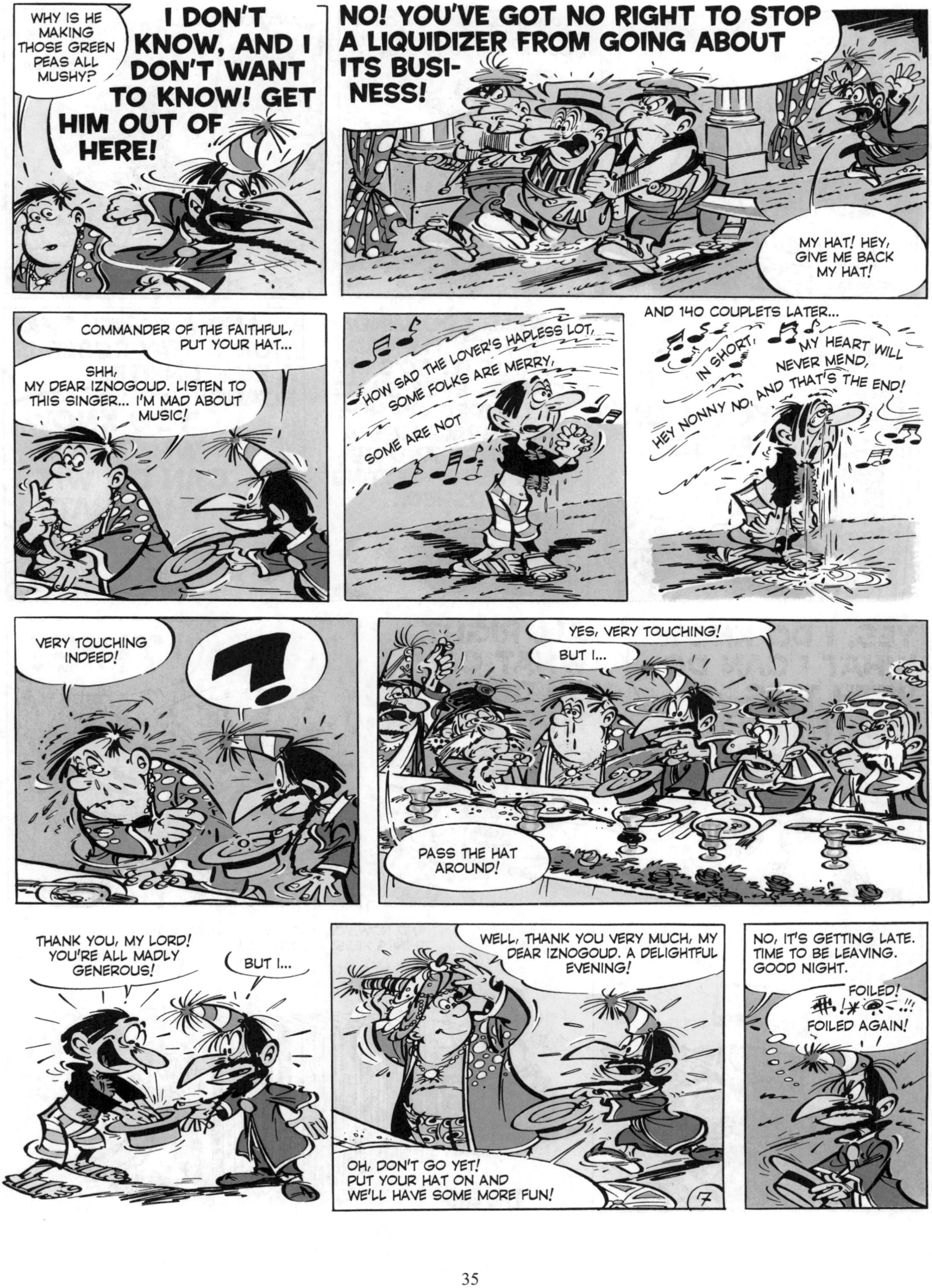
WHY IS HE MAKING THOSE GREEN PEAS ALL MUSHY?
I DON'T KNOW, AND I DON'T WANT TO KNOW! GET HIM OUT OF HERE!
NO! YOU'VE GOT NO RIGHT TO STOP A LIQUIDIZER FROM GOING ABOUT ITS BUSI-NESS!
MY HAT! HEY, GIVE ME BACK MY HAT!
COMMANDER OF THE FAITHFUL, PUT YOUR HAT...
SHH, MY DEAR IZNOGOUD. LISTEN TO THIS SINGER... I'M MAD ABOUT MUSIC!
HOW SAD THE LOVER'S HAPLESS LOT, SOME FOLKS ARE MERRY, SOME ARE NOT
AND 140 COUPLETS LATER...
IN SHORT, MY HEART WILL NEVER MEND, HEY NONNY NO, AND THAT'S THE END!
VERY TOUCHING INDEED!
?
YES, VERY TOUCHING!
BUT I...
PASS THE HAT AROUND!
THANK YOU, MY LORD! YOU'RE ALL MADLY GENEROUS!
BUT I...
WELL, THANK YOU VERY MUCH, MY DEAR IZNOGOUD. A DELIGHTFUL EVENING!
OH, DON'T GO YET! PUT YOUR HAT ON AND WE'LL HAVE SOME MORE FUN!
NO, IT'S GETTING LATE. TIME TO BE LEAVING. GOOD NIGHT.
FOILED!
FOILED AGAIN!

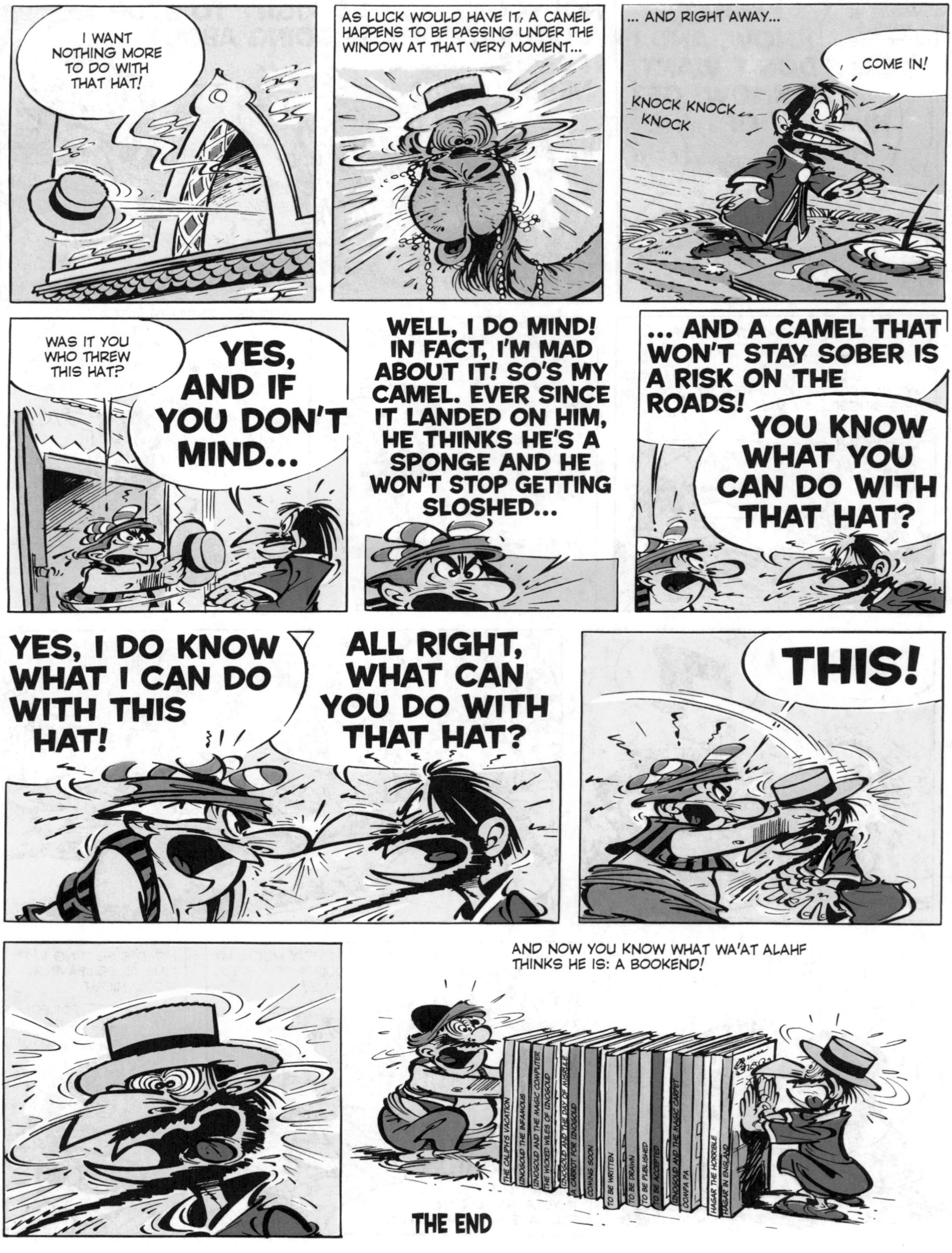
I WANT NOTHING MORE TO DO WITH THAT HAT!
AS LUCK WOULD HAVE IT, A CAMEL HAPPENS TO BE PASSING UNDER THE WINDOW AT THAT VERY MOMENT...
... AND RIGHT AWAY...
KNOCK KNOCK KNOCK
COME IN!
WAS IT YOU WHO THREW THIS HAT?
YES, AND IF YOU DON'T MIND...
WELL, I DO MIND! IN FACT, I'M MAD ABOUT IT! SO'S MY CAMEL. EVER SINCE IT LANDED ON HIM, HE THINKS HE'S A SPONGE AND HE WON'T STOP GETTING SLOSHED...
... AND A CAMEL THAT WON'T STAY SOBER IS A RISK ON THE ROADS!
YOU KNOW WHAT YOU CAN DO WITH THAT HAT?
YES, I DO KNOW WHAT I CAN DO WITH THIS HAT!
ALL RIGHT, WHAT CAN YOU DO WITH THAT HAT?
THIS!
AND NOW YOU KNOW WHAT WA'AT ALAHF THINKS HE IS: A BOOKEND!
THE CALIPH'S VACATION
IZNOGOUD THE INFAMOUS
IZNOGOUD AND THE MAGIC COMPUTER
THE WICKED WILES OF IZNOGOUD
IZNOGOUD AND THE DAY OF MISRULE
A CARROT FOR IZNOGOUD
COMING SOON
TO BE WRITTEN
TO BE DRAWN
TO BE PUBLISHED
TO BE ACCEPTED
IZNOGOUD AND THE MAGIC CARPET
OOMPA PA
HAGAR THE HORRIBLE
HAGAR IN ENGLAND
THE END

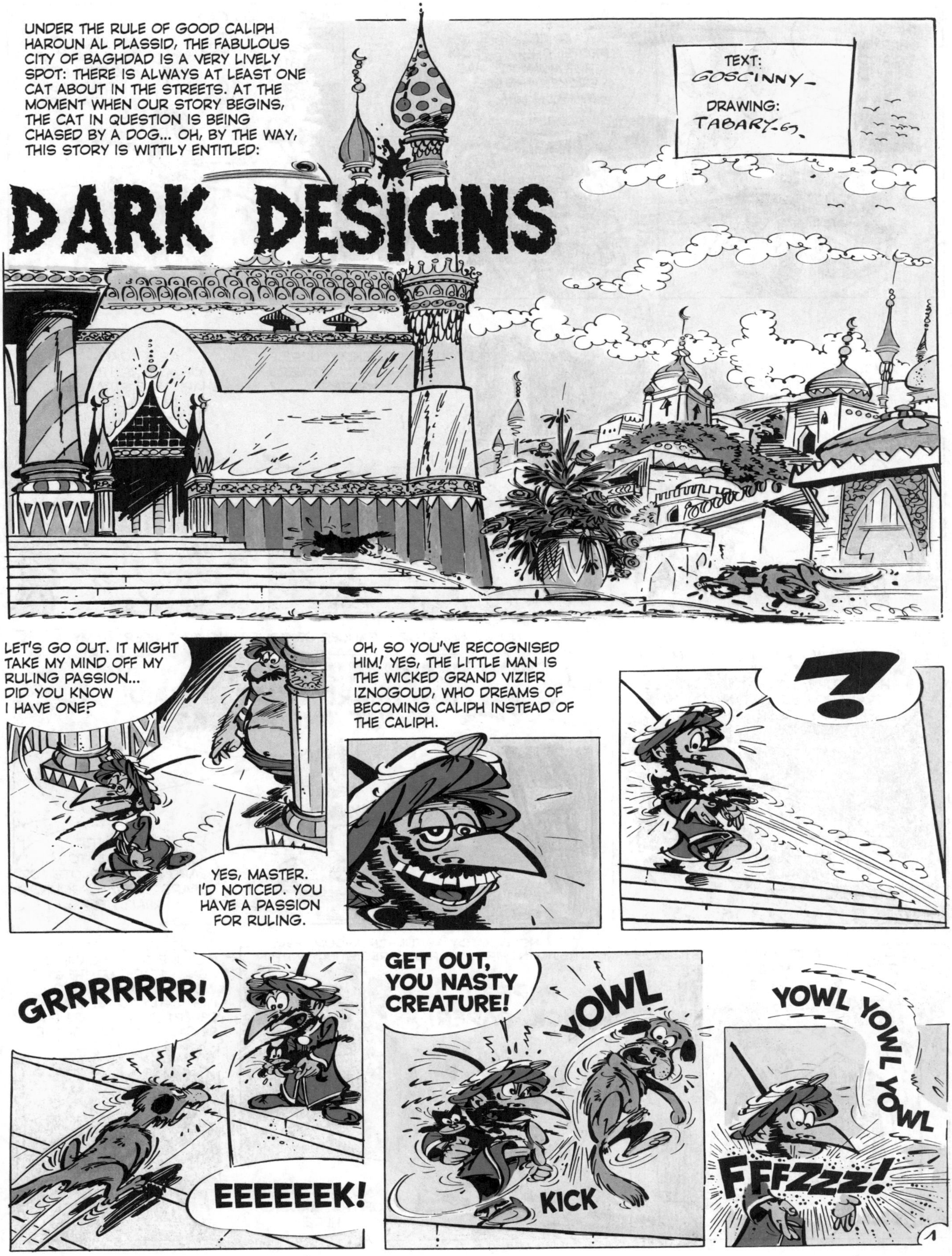
UNDER THE RULE OF GOOD CALIPH HAROUN AL PLASSID, THE FABULOUS CITY OF BAGHDAD IS A VERY LIVELY SPOT: THERE IS ALWAYS AT LEAST ONE CAT ABOUT IN THE STREETS. AT THE MOMENT WHEN OUR STORY BEGINS, THE CAT IN QUESTION IS BEING CHASED BY A DOG... OH, BY THE WAY, THIS STORY IS WITTILY ENTITLED:
TEXT: GOSCINNY
DRAWING: TABARY
DARK DESIGNS
LET'S GO OUT. IT MIGHT TAKE MY MIND OFF MY RULING PASSION... DID YOU KNOW I HAVE ONE?
YES, MASTER. I'D NOTICED. YOU HAVE A PASSION FOR RULING.
OH, SO YOU'VE RECOGNISED HIM! YES, THE LITTLE MAN IS THE WICKED GRAND VIZIER IZNOGOUD, WHO DREAMS OF BECOMING CALIPH INSTEAD OF THE CALIPH.
?
GRRRRRRR!
EEEEEEK!
GET OUT, YOU NASTY CREATURE!
YOWL
KICK
YOWL YOWL YOWL YOWL
FFFZZZ!
1

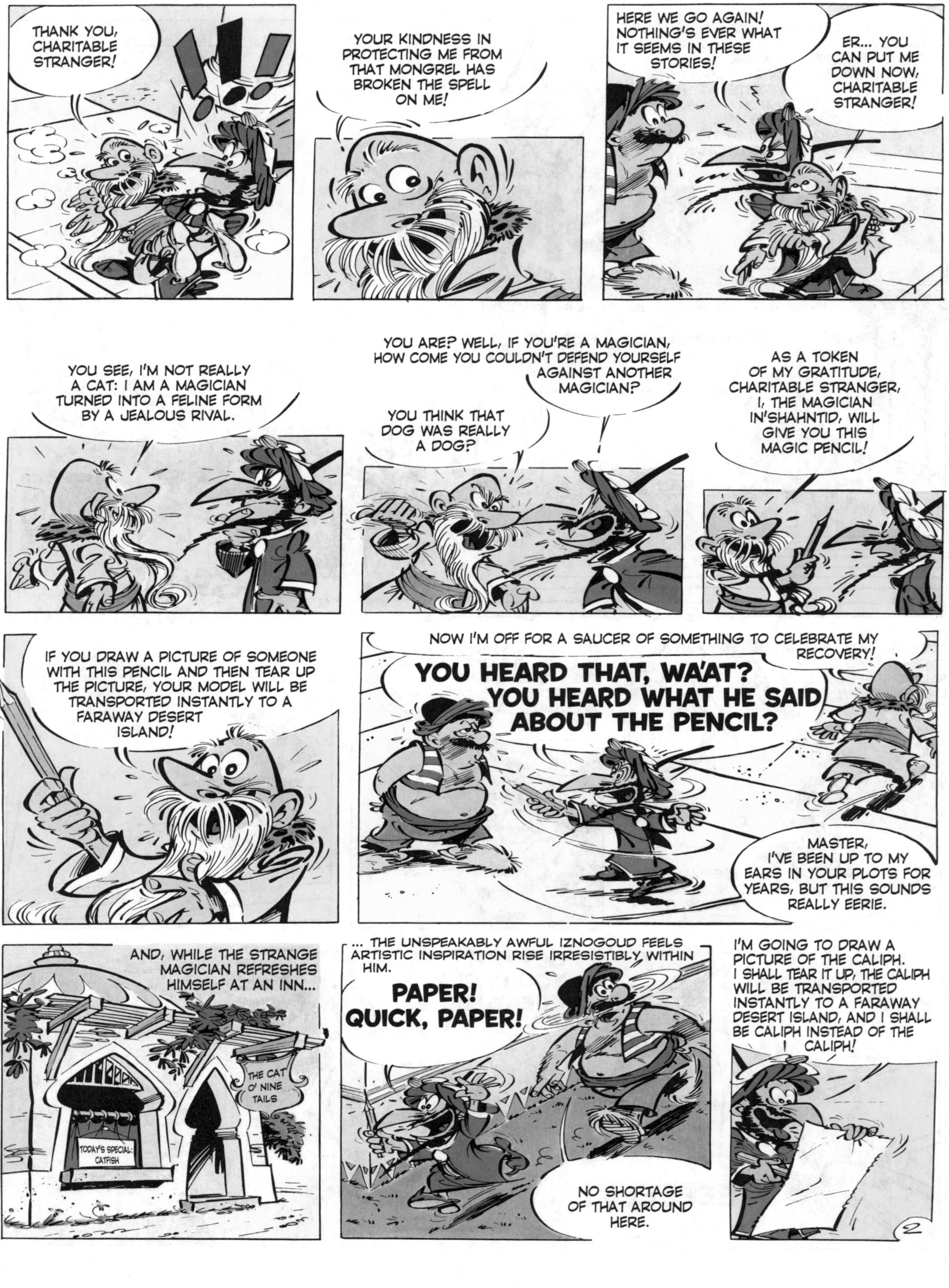

THANK YOU, CHARITABLE STRANGER!
YOUR KINDNESS IN PROTECTING ME FROM THAT MONGREL HAS BROKEN THE SPELL ON ME!
HERE WE GO AGAIN! NOTHING'S EVER WHAT IT SEEMS IN THESE STORIES!
ER... YOU CAN PUT ME DOWN NOW, CHARITABLE STRANGER!
YOU SEE, I'M NOT REALLY A CAT: I AM A MAGICIAN TURNED INTO A FELINE FORM BY A JEALOUS RIVAL.
YOU ARE? WELL, IF YOU'RE A MAGICIAN, HOW COME YOU COULDN'T DEFEND YOURSELF AGAINST ANOTHER MAGICIAN?
YOU THINK THAT DOG WAS REALLY A DOG?
AS A TOKEN OF MY GRATITUDE, CHARITABLE STRANGER, I, THE MAGICIAN IN'SHAHNTID, WILL GIVE YOU THIS MAGIC PENCIL!
IF YOU DRAW A PICTURE OF SOMEONE WITH THIS PENCIL AND THEN TEAR UP THE PICTURE, YOUR MODEL WILL BE TRANSPORTED INSTANTLY TO A FARAWAY DESERT ISLAND!
NOW I'M OFF FOR A SAUCER OF SOMETHING TO CELEBRATE MY RECOVERY!
YOU HEARD THAT, WA'AT? YOU HEARD WHAT HE SAID ABOUT THE PENCIL?
MASTER, I'VE BEEN UP TO MY EARS IN YOUR PLOTS FOR YEARS, BUT THIS SOUNDS REALLY EERIE.
AND, WHILE THE STRANGE MAGICIAN REFRESHES HIMSELF AT AN INN...
THE CAT O' NINE TAILS
TODAY'S SPECIAL: CATFISH
... THE UNSPEAKABLY AWFUL IZNOGOUD FEELS ARTISTIC INSPIRATION RISE IRRESISTIBLY WITHIN HIM.
PAPER! QUICK, PAPER!
NO SHORTAGE OF THAT AROUND HERE.
I'M GOING TO DRAW A PICTURE OF THE CALIPH. I SHALL TEAR IT UP, THE CALIPH WILL BE TRANSPORTED INSTANTLY TO A FARAWAY DESERT ISLAND, AND I SHALL BE CALIPH INSTEAD OF THE CALIPH!
2

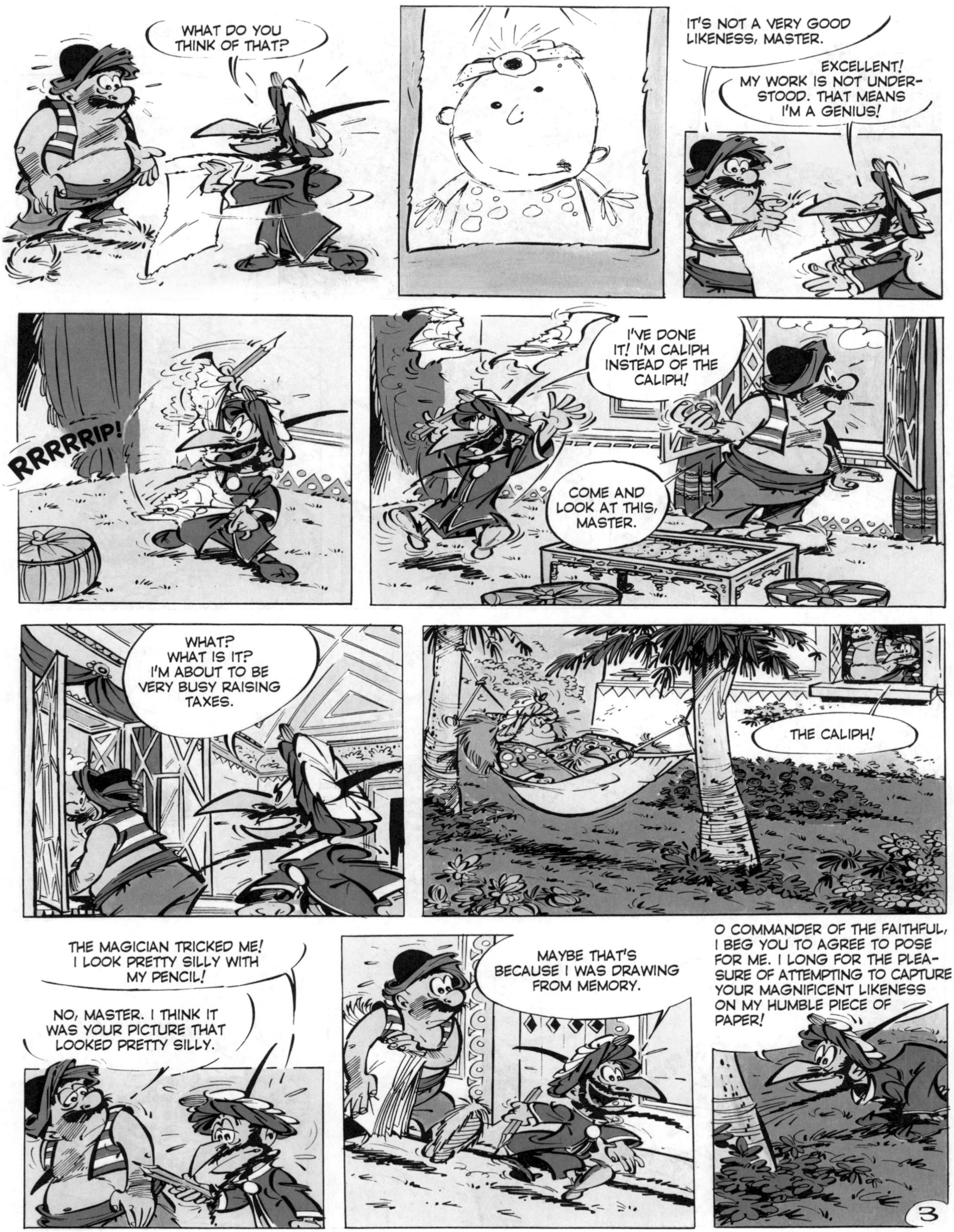
WHAT DO YOU THINK OF THAT?
IT'S NOT A VERY GOOD LIKENESS, MASTER.
EXCELLENT! MY WORK IS NOT UNDER-STOOD. THAT MEANS I'M A GENIUS!
RRRRRIP!
I'VE DONE IT! I'M CALIPH INSTEAD OF THE CALIPH!
COME AND LOOK AT THIS, MASTER.
WHAT? WHAT IS IT? I'M ABOUT TO BE VERY BUSY RAISING TAXES.
THE CALIPH!
THE MAGICIAN TRICKED ME! I LOOK PRETTY SILLY WITH MY PENCIL!
NO, MASTER. I THINK IT WAS YOUR PICTURE THAT LOOKED PRETTY SILLY.
MAYBE THAT'S BECAUSE I WAS DRAWING FROM MEMORY.
O COMMANDER OF THE FAITHFUL, I BEG YOU TO AGREE TO POSE FOR ME. I LONG FOR THE PLEA-SURE OF ATTEMPTING TO CAPTURE YOUR MAGNIFICENT LIKENESS ON MY HUMBLE PIECE OF PAPER!
3

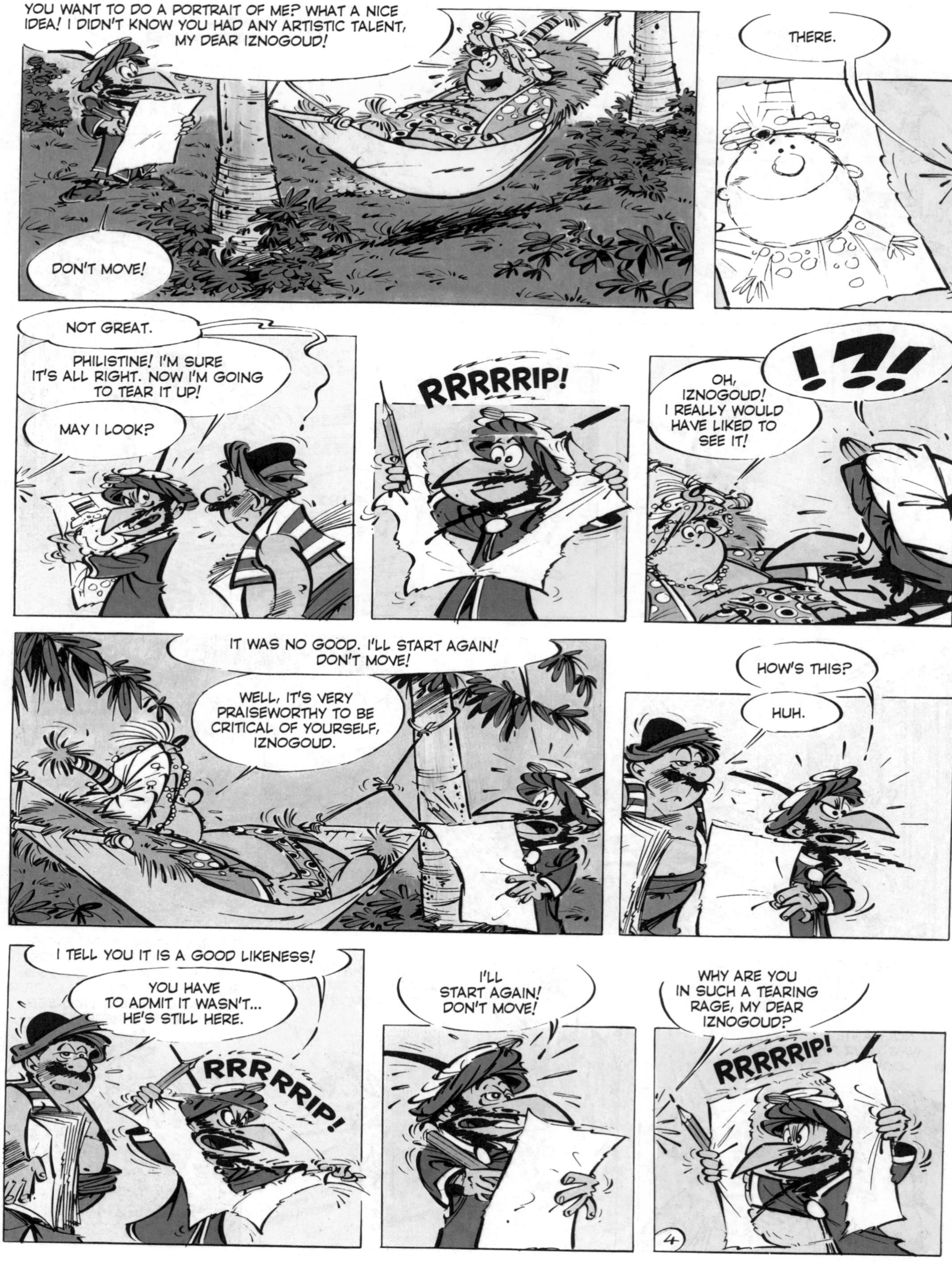
YOU WANT TO DO A PORTRAIT OF ME? WHAT A NICE IDEA! I DIDN'T KNOW YOU HAD ANY ARTISTIC TALENT, MY DEAR IZNOGOUD!
DON'T MOVE!
THERE.
NOT GREAT.
PHILISTINE! I'M SURE IT'S ALL RIGHT. NOW I'M GOING TO TEAR IT UP!
MAY I LOOK?
RRRRRIP!
OH, IZNOGOUD! I REALLY WOULD HAVE LIKED TO SEE IT!
!?!
IT WAS NO GOOD. I'LL START AGAIN! DON'T MOVE!
WELL, IT'S VERY PRAISEWORTHY TO BE CRITICAL OF YOURSELF, IZNOGOUD.
HOW'S THIS?
HUH.
I TELL YOU IT IS A GOOD LIKENESS!
YOU HAVE TO ADMIT IT WASN'T... HE'S STILL HERE.
RRRRRIP!
I'LL START AGAIN! DON'T MOVE!
WHY ARE YOU IN SUCH A TEARING RAGE, MY DEAR IZNOGOUD?
RRRRRIP!
4

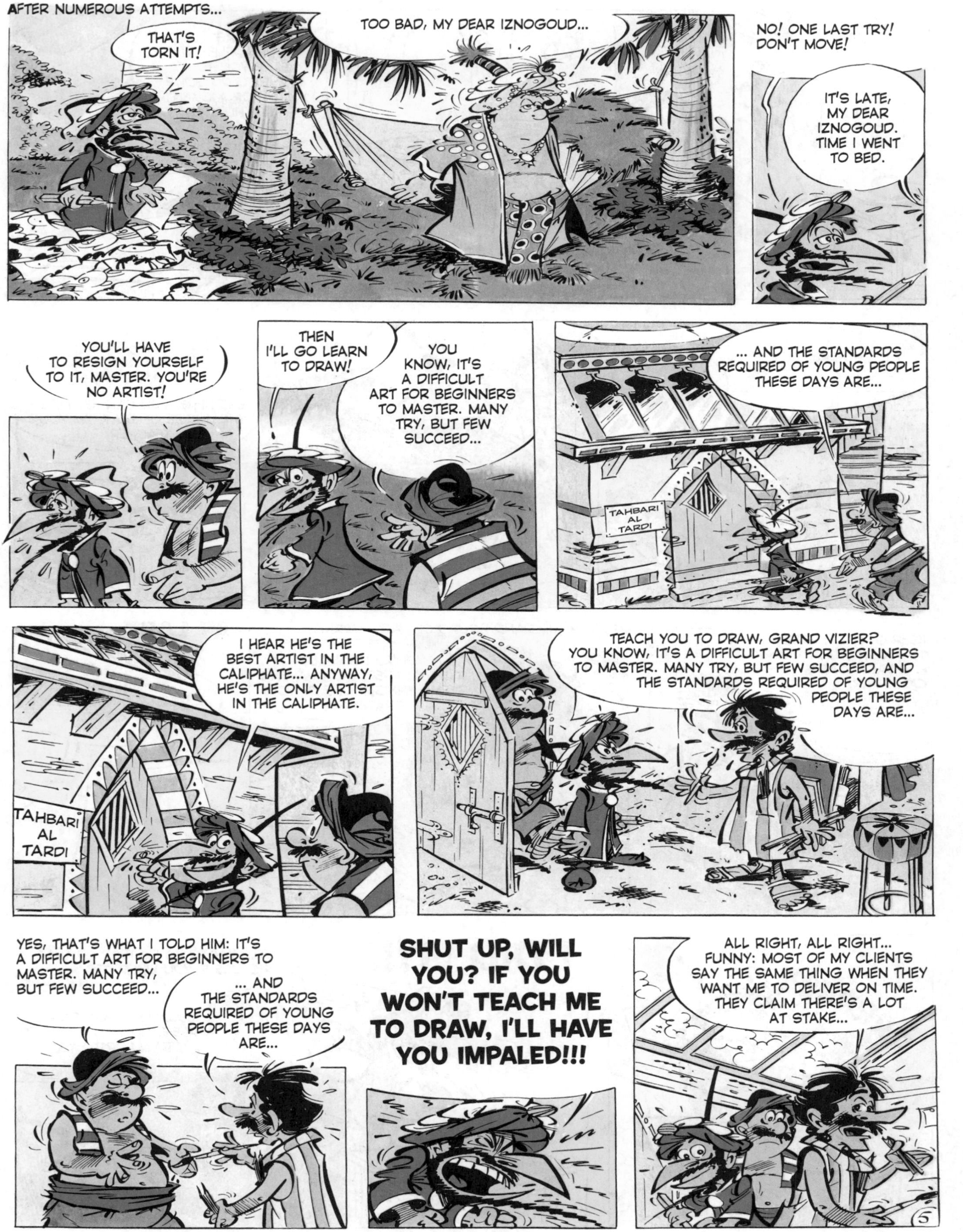
AFTER NUMEROUS ATTEMPTS...
THAT'S TORN IT!
TOO BAD, MY DEAR IZNOGOUD...
NO! ONE LAST TRY! DON'T MOVE!
IT'S LATE, MY DEAR IZNOGOUD. TIME I WENT TO BED.
YOU'LL HAVE TO RESIGN YOURSELF TO IT, MASTER. YOU'RE NO ARTIST!
THEN I'LL GO LEARN TO DRAW!
YOU KNOW, IT'S A DIFFICULT ART FOR BEGINNERS TO MASTER. MANY TRY, BUT FEW SUCCEED...
... AND THE STANDARDS REQUIRED OF YOUNG PEOPLE THESE DAYS ARE...
TAHBARI AL TARDI
I HEAR HE'S THE BEST ARTIST IN THE CALIPHATE... ANYWAY, HE'S THE ONLY ARTIST IN THE CALIPHATE.
TAHBARI AL TARDI
TEACH YOU TO DRAW, GRAND VIZIER? YOU KNOW, IT'S A DIFFICULT ART FOR BEGINNERS TO MASTER. MANY TRY, BUT FEW SUCCEED, AND THE STANDARDS REQUIRED OF YOUNG PEOPLE THESE DAYS ARE...
YES, THAT'S WHAT I TOLD HIM: IT'S A DIFFICULT ART FOR BEGINNERS TO MASTER. MANY TRY, BUT FEW SUCCEED...
... AND THE STANDARDS REQUIRED OF YOUNG PEOPLE THESE DAYS ARE...
SHUT UP, WILL YOU? IF YOU WON'T TEACH ME TO DRAW, I'LL HAVE YOU IMPALED!!!
ALL RIGHT, ALL RIGHT... FUNNY: MOST OF MY CLIENTS SAY THE SAME THING WHEN THEY WANT ME TO DELIVER ON TIME. THEY CLAIM THERE'S A LOT AT STAKE...
5

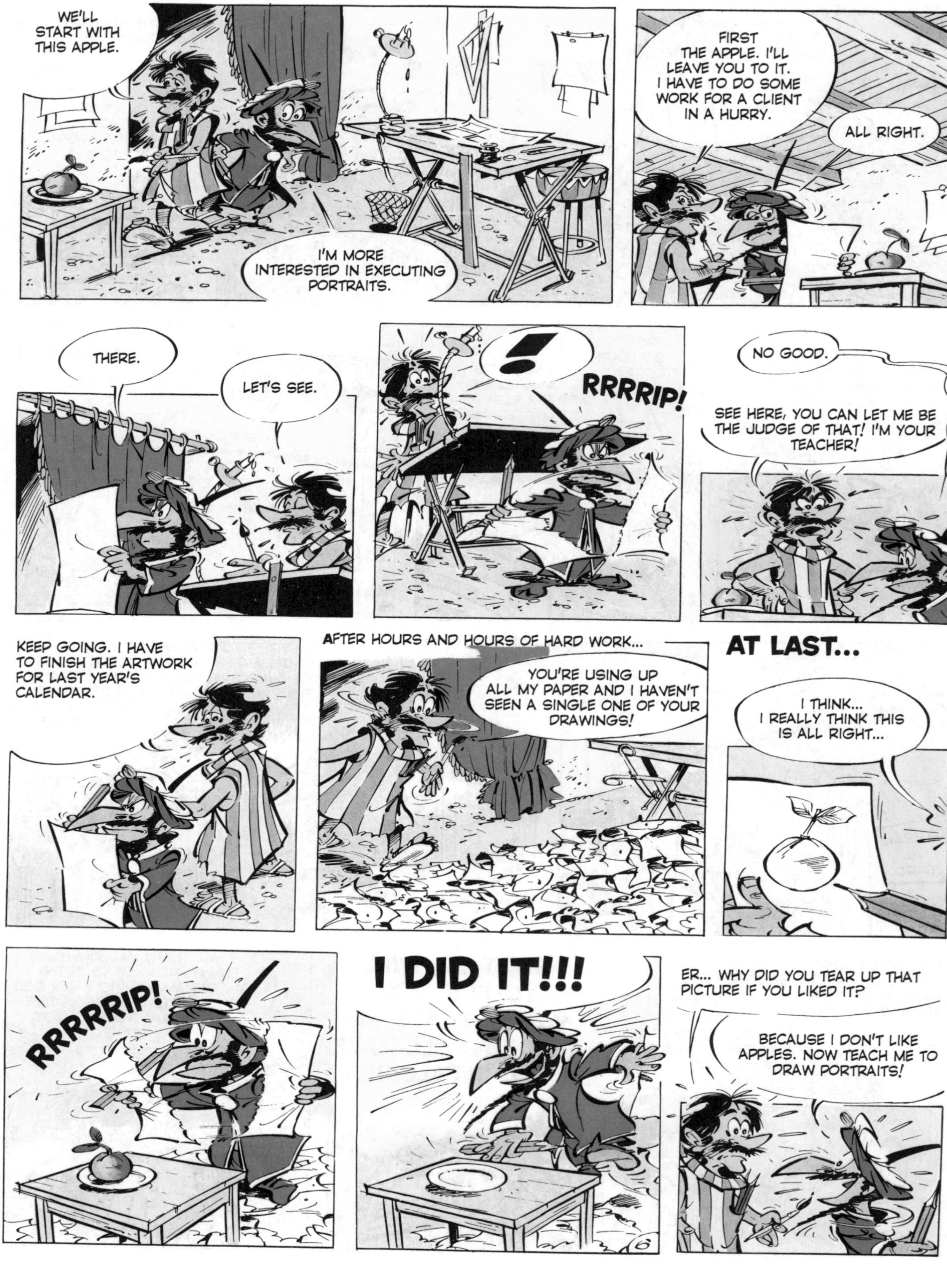
WE'LL START WITH THIS APPLE.
I'M MORE INTERESTED IN EXECUTING PORTRAITS.
FIRST THE APPLE. I'LL LEAVE YOU TO IT. I HAVE TO DO SOME WORK FOR A CLIENT IN A HURRY.
ALL RIGHT.
THERE.
LET'S SEE.
!
RRRRIP!
NO GOOD.
SEE HERE, YOU CAN LET ME BE THE JUDGE OF THAT! I'M YOUR TEACHER!
KEEP GOING. I HAVE TO FINISH THE ARTWORK FOR LAST YEAR'S CALENDAR.
AFTER HOURS AND HOURS OF HARD WORK...
YOU'RE USING UP ALL MY PAPER AND I HAVEN'T SEEN A SINGLE ONE OF YOUR DRAWINGS!
AT LAST...
I THINK... I REALLY THINK THIS IS ALL RIGHT...
RRRRRIP!
I DID IT!!!
ER... WHY DID YOU TEAR UP THAT PICTURE IF YOU LIKED IT?
BECAUSE I DON'T LIKE APPLES. NOW TEACH ME TO DRAW PORTRAITS!

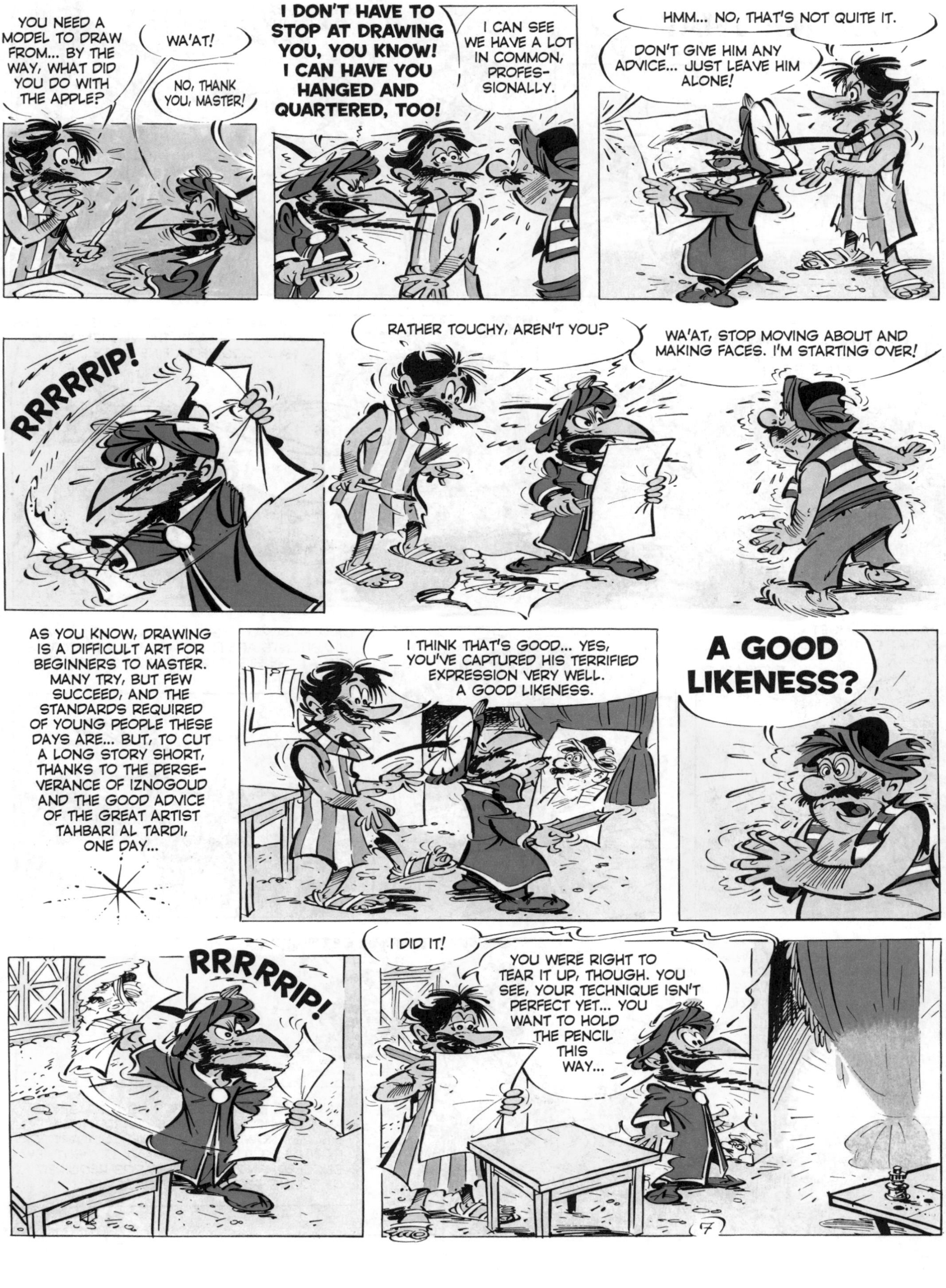

YOU NEED A MODEL TO DRAW FROM... BY THE WAY, WHAT DID YOU DO WITH THE APPLE?
WA'AT!
NO, THANK YOU, MASTER!
I DON'T HAVE TO STOP AT DRAWING YOU, YOU KNOW! I CAN HAVE YOU HANGED AND QUARTERED, TOO!
I CAN SEE WE HAVE A LOT IN COMMON, PROFES-SIONALLY.
HMM... NO, THAT'S NOT QUITE IT.
DON'T GIVE HIM ANY ADVICE... JUST LEAVE HIM ALONE!
RRRRRIP!
RATHER TOUCHY, AREN'T YOU?
WA'AT, STOP MOVING ABOUT AND MAKING FACES. I'M STARTING OVER!
AS YOU KNOW, DRAWING IS A DIFFICULT ART FOR BEGINNERS TO MASTER. MANY TRY, BUT FEW SUCCEED, AND THE STANDARDS REQUIRED OF YOUNG PEOPLE THESE DAYS ARE... BUT, TO CUT A LONG STORY SHORT, THANKS TO THE PERSE-VERANCE OF IZNOGOUD AND THE GOOD ADVICE OF THE GREAT ARTIST TAHBARI AL TARDI, ONE DAY...
I THINK THAT'S GOOD... YES, YOU'VE CAPTURED HIS TERRIFIED EXPRESSION VERY WELL. A GOOD LIKENESS.
A GOOD LIKENESS?
RRRRRIP!
I DID IT!
YOU WERE RIGHT TO TEAR IT UP, THOUGH. YOU SEE, YOUR TECHNIQUE ISN'T PERFECT YET... YOU WANT TO HOLD THE PENCIL THIS WAY...
7

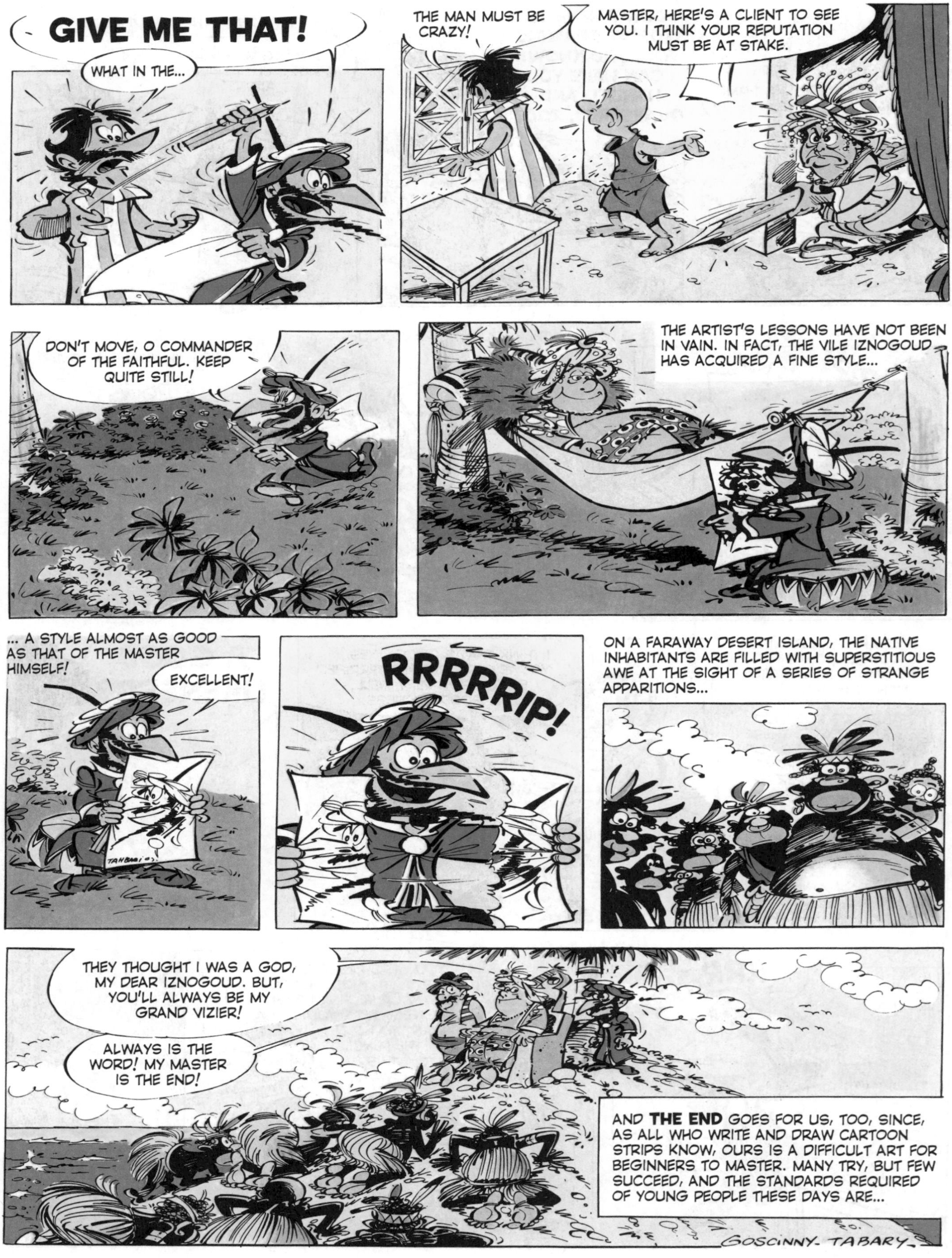
GIVE ME THAT!
WHAT IN THE...
THE MAN MUST BE CRAZY!
MASTER, HERE'S A CLIENT TO SEE YOU. I THINK YOUR REPUTATION MUST BE AT STAKE.
DON'T MOVE, O COMMANDER OF THE FAITHFUL. KEEP QUITE STILL!
THE ARTIST'S LESSONS HAVE NOT BEEN IN VAIN. IN FACT, THE VILE IZNOGOUD HAS ACQUIRED A FINE STYLE...
... A STYLE ALMOST AS GOOD AS THAT OF THE MASTER HIMSELF!
EXCELLENT!
RRRRRRIP!
ON A FARAWAY DESERT ISLAND, THE NATIVE INHABITANTS ARE FILLED WITH SUPERSTITIOUS AWE AT THE SIGHT OF A SERIES OF STRANGE APPARITIONS...
THEY THOUGHT I WAS A GOD, MY DEAR IZNOGOUD. BUT, YOU'LL ALWAYS BE MY GRAND VIZIER!
ALWAYS IS THE WORD! MY MASTER IS THE END!
AND THE END GOES FOR US, TOO, SINCE, AS ALL WHO WRITE AND DRAW CARTOON STRIPS KNOW, OURS IS A DIFFICULT ART FOR BEGINNERS TO MASTER. MANY TRY, BUT FEW SUCCEED, AND THE STANDARDS REQUIRED OF YOUNG PEOPLE THESE DAYS ARE...
GOSCINNY-TABARY

# IZNOGOUD

GOSCINNY - TABARY
THE WICKED WILES OF
IZNOGOUD

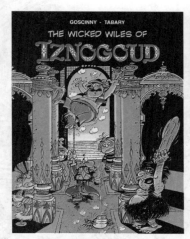

1 - THE WICKED WILES OF IZNOGOUD

GOSCINNY - TABARY
IZNOGOUD
THE CALIPH'S
VACATION

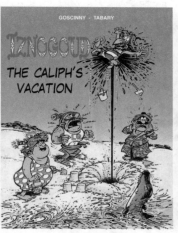

2 - THE CALIPH'S VACATION

GOSCINNY - TABARY
IZNOGOUD
AND
THE DAY
OF MISRULE

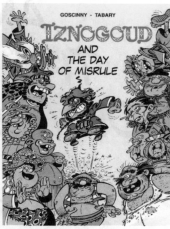

3 - IZNOGOUD AND THE DAY OF MISRULE

GOSCINNY - TABARY
IZNOGOUD
AND THE MAGIC COMPUTER

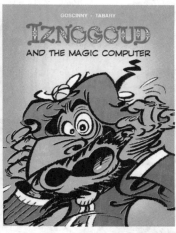

4 - IZNOGOUD AND THE MAGIC COMPUTER

GOSCINNY - TABARY
A CARROT
FOR
IZNOGOUD

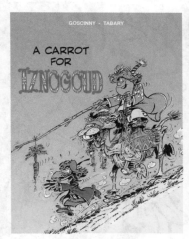

5 - A CARROT FOR IZNOGOUD

GOSCINNY - TABARY
IZNOGOUD
AND THE
MAGIC CARPET

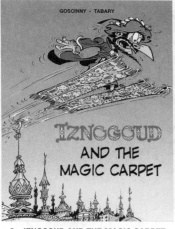

6 - IZNOGOUD AND THE MAGIC CARPET

GOSCINNY - TABARY
IZNOGOUD
THE INFAMOUS

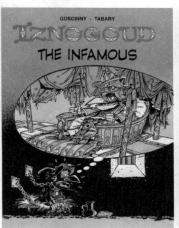

7 - IZNOGOUD THE INFAMOUS

GOSCINNY - TABARY
IZNOGOUD
ROCKETS TO
STARDOM

8 - IZNOGOUD ROCKETS TO STARDOM

9th CINEBOOK
The 9th Art Publisher
www.cinebook.com

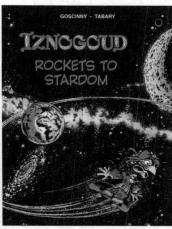

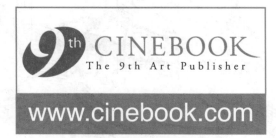

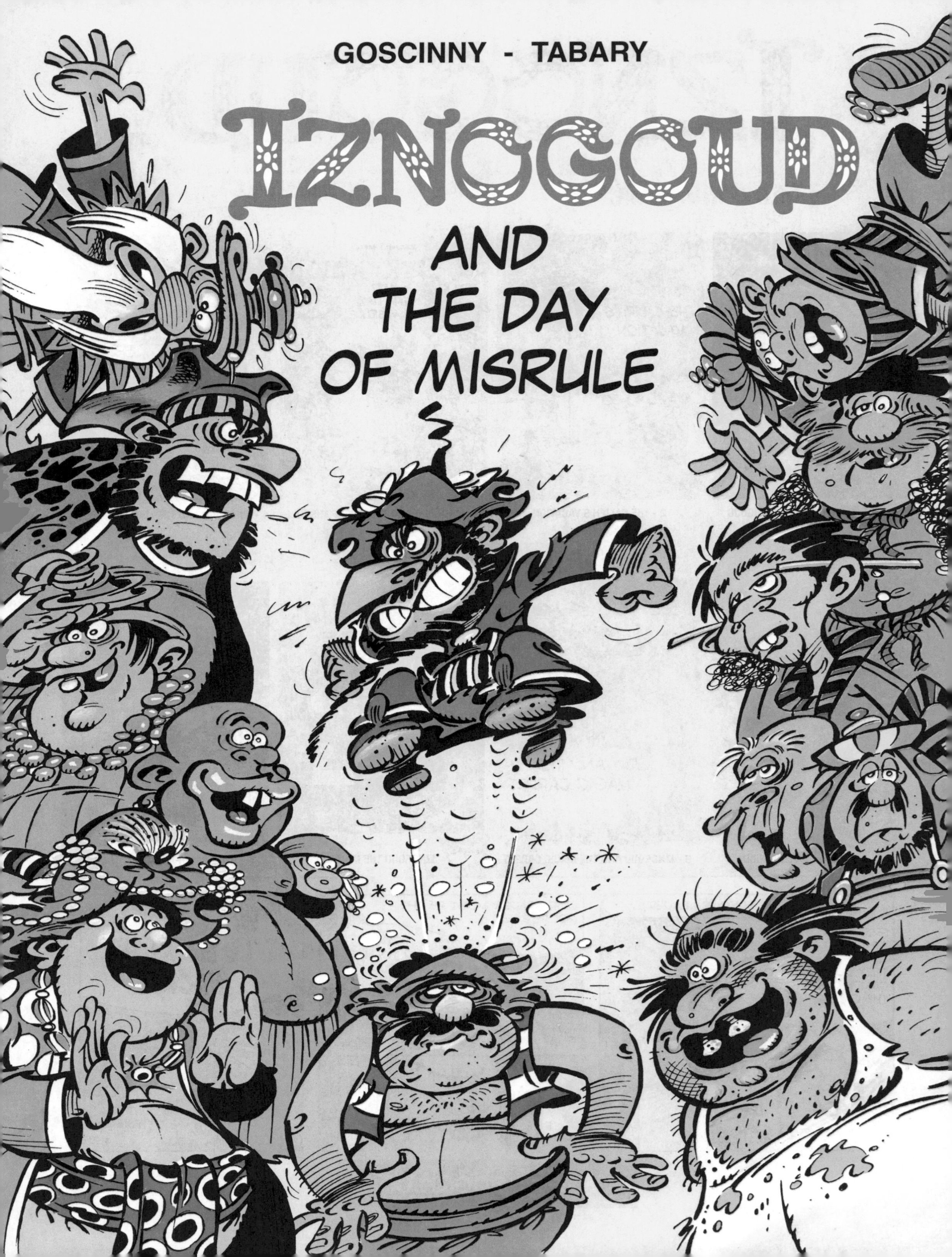
GOSCINNY - TABARY
IZNOGOUD
AND
THE DAY
OF MISRULE

9 PM

BROTHERS! TODAY IS THE DAY OF MISRULE! IN A FEW HOURS' TIME, HOWEVER, THINGS WILL BE BACK TO NORMAL, AND HAROUN AL PLASSID WILL BE CALIPH ONCE AGAIN!

BROTHERS, WILL YOU ALLOW YOURSELVES TO COME UNDER THE YOKE OF TYRANNY AGAIN... CONTINUE TO OBEY THE ELITIST ARISTOCRATS AND INTELLECTUALS?

NO!

HE'S RIGHT!

NO MORE YOLKS! NO MORE EGGHEADS!

LET US GET RID OF HAROUN AL PLASSID, AND EVERY DAY WILL BE A DAY OF MISRULE!

YEAH!

DEATH TO THE TYRANT!

YEAH!

THEN, FOLLOW ME!

WHY SHOULD WE FOLLOW YOU?

BE... BECAUSE I'M YOUR LEADER!

PRECISELY. ON THE DAY OF MISRULE, LEADERS DON'T LEAD—THEY FOLLOW... AND THEY DON'T GET TO BE CALIPH INSTEAD OF THE CALIPH!

OUR LEADER MUST BE THE POOREST OF US ALL!

YEAH, AND YOU'RE IZNOGOUD THE RICH!

WAIT HERE! I'LL BE RIGHT BACK!

17

IZNOGOUD AND THE DAY OF MISRULE

# IZNOGOUD

## COMING SOON

GOSCINNY - TABARY
THE GRAND VIZIER
IZNOGOUD
TABARY

**9 - THE GRAND VIZIER IZNOGOUD**

GOSCINNY - TABARY
IZNOGOUD
THE RELENTLESS

**10 - IZNOGOUD THE RELENTLESS**

9th CINEBOOK
The 9th Art Publisher
www.cinebook.com